Shelley Kassian

The Half Mile
of Baby Blue

ALSO BY SHELLEY KASSIAN

Fantasy

The Odin Saga:

The Scarlett Mark, Book 1

The Ebony Queen, Book 2

Contemporary Romance

The Thurston Hotel Series:

A Lasting Harmony, Book 5

Historical Romance

A Sacrifice for Love

A Heart Across the Ocean

The Half Mile of Baby Blue

A WOMEN OF STAMPEDE NOVEL

SHELLEY KASSIAN

Published 2018 by Shelley Kassian
(shelleykassian.com)

ISBN: 978-0-9959680-5-9 (Print edition)

Design and cover art by Su Kopil, Earthly Charms
Copyediting by Ted Williams

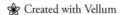 Created with Vellum

DEDICATION

I dedicate The Half Mile of Baby Blue to my adult children.
—Carrie and William, Shawn, and Alicia and Trevor—
I thought of you often while writing this book.
I'm grateful you're a part of my life.
I appreciate the noise you make;
The joy, the love, especially the laughter!
I love you...
I'm richer in words because of your exploits!

FOREWORD

I had the privilege of reading an advance copy of *The Half Mile of Baby Blue*. Touching, heartwarming and real, this novel pulls you into the Wheeler family's life. Hidden legacies, conflicting values and a personal half-mile of hell. Take a breathtaking ride with Kit Wheeler and her new love, Gabe Bradshaw, as they race to find love and save the family ranch.

Katie O'Connor, author of the contemporary Heart's Haven series; Building Trust, Running Home, and Saving Grace.

PREFACE

The Half Mile of Baby Blue was written to celebrate The Greatest Outdoor Show on Earth–The Calgary Stampede. The Stampede stages ten days of entertainment, where Calgarians and visitors alike partake of exhibitions, midway, star attractions, and Western-themed events. The Calgary Stampede is especially known for the rodeo, an important part of Calgary's heritage.

In writing this story, I was drawn to the rodeo, and in particular, the chuckwagons. In my research, I hope I gained a better understanding and respect for the drivers, outriders, helpers and families who love this Western sport.

A crew travels between Alberta and Saskatchewan from May to August with few breaks in between races. Imagine as I did, the Stampede circuit and the first race of the season: The Grande Prairie Stompede.

My intent as an author was always to have my fictional rodeo family, 'the Wheelers,' participate at the Calgary Stampede in a way that was believable to readers but also paid proper homage to the sport. Does my family possess the skills to race at The Calgary Stampede? Maybe yes, and maybe… no. But as in life, it doesn't matter so much how we arrive at our destination, or the skills a person holds. None of us are excluded from education, hard work, or training.

My story is more so about the distance a family must go to realize their history and purpose, and what they're prepared to do, *as a family*, to arrive at their destination.

It doesn't matter who wins or loses. Like Eddie the Eagle or the Jamaican Bobsled team, what's important is having the will to try!

The Calgary Stampede's first exhibition happened in 1886. A period in Calgary's history when the city was no more than a small town. The exhibition was an opportunity to share knowledge about agriculture, celebrating Western culture and showcasing the best of the West. Founded by American promoter, Guy Weadick in 1912, the Exhibition became an annual event in 1923, when it merged with the Calgary Industrial Exhibition to create the Calgary Exhibition and Stampede. This was also the first year chuckwagons raced the half mile of Hell.

I have lived in Calgary most of my adult life. I've raised my family in this caring community. I appreciate how the people of Calgary respond to life, and the Stampede. You feel the vibe as Calgarians dawn their Western gear, at work and at play, partaking of pancake breakfasts and visiting the Stampede grounds.

If you're ever in Calgary the first week of July, come on by. Saddle up for the ride. You're sure to have a good time!

ACKNOWLEDGMENTS

I wish to thank *The Half Mile of Baby Blue* contributors who supported either the research or the writing of this novel.

The first draft was in fairly good shape, but my beta readers: Alyssa Linn Palmer, Katie O'Connor and Brenda Sinclair, assisted in fashioning this book into a work of art. I hope it's a work of Western art!

I didn't know much about the Western sport of chuckwagon racing or the thoroughbred horses required to pull the wagons, beyond the knowledge of watching the sport as a spectator. I wish to thank Kathy Bartley of Bear Valley Rescue for her knowledge of rescue horses. I also thank Kirsten Neumann Stephens, an ambassador for Go and Play Stable in Ontario, for her further assistance with horse knowledge.

I had a vision to write about the Greatest Outdoor Show on Earth, The Calgary Stampede. I thank my planning partner extraordinaire, Katie O'Connor, who held the reins and managed this project from the beginning to the end, supporting me and a team of six other writers in every way imaginable. A shout out to Brenda Sinclair with her knowledge of The Thurston Hotel series, who entered the management team once the project was well underway, sharpening her blue pencil, and ~~assisting with~~ critiquing the entire series, for ~~which I shall~~ be eternally grateful!

Seven local Alberta authors collaborated and contributed to the Women of Stampede series: Maeve Buchanan, C.G. Furst, Katie O'Connor, Alyssa Linn Palmer, Brenda Sinclair and Nicole Roy. This spectacular series would not have been possible without you! It's been a wild ride and I thank each of you for sharing it with me!

Finally, I thank my family, and especially my adult children for supporting my publishing efforts! These kids at heart have explored many exploits in their lives, so a mother does have stories to tell. But I assure you, the stories inside this book are born of an author's imagination and are fictional!

CHAPTER 1

*K*it Wheeler couldn't comprehend the news her father had shared with the family. Misfortune happened to other people, not the Wheelers, but she could see by her dad's somber expression, the sad timbre of his voice, that every word was true. The bank had threatened to foreclose. But she wouldn't lose their family home without a fight.

"How much time do we have to save the ranch? I have money set aside. I can help."

Kit sat on an armchair in the corner of the living room feeling estranged from her family. The distance irritated her. She willed one of her siblings, her parents, or her grandmother, to speak— Silence. Defeat.

Her grandmother swayed back and forth on her old rocking chair as if waiting for death to come, or maybe the situation angered her. Kit couldn't tell.

"Come on," Kit begged, looking at each family member in turn, "will no one say anything?"

Sitting on a worn, gray-leather sofa, her father folded his arms. "Look, Kit, it's great you want to help, but I'm not sure I can let you. Your funds probably wouldn't make a difference anyway."

"It's worse than you're saying, isn't it?" She stretched forward, crossing her legs at her ankles. "Or could it be you won't take my money, won't accept my help? Dad. Why did you call us here? Will you throw your cards on the table, folding, admitting ruin, or at least try to play another round?"

"I won't give up without a fight if that's what you're asking. I don't like losing."

"Just tell us, then. The truth. We're adults. We can accept whatever you have to say."

"You're right. We're behind on our mortgage payments by three months," Michael Wheeler said, sighing. "The bank wants their money, but they're willing to negotiate terms to give us more time. I've been in contact with a senior financial advisor. He's suggesting we sell."

Kit scrutinized her mom, her sister, Samantha, her brother, Cole. Not one useful piece of advice was put forward. She'd have to push them for the truth.

"What do you think about this situation, Sam, Cole? Surely, you don't want to sell?"

"Not me," Cole remarked, his palms massaging his Wranglers. "But it's not my decision to make."

"I love it here," Gina Wheeler added, a wistful smile appearing on her face. "I can't imagine living anywhere else. Fresh air, blue skies, and the mountains in the distance. We've put in a lot of work to create a garden landscape by the pond. And you know how I love painting in the midst of the flowers in the heat of summer. I'd miss it, like I miss my daughter."

"Oh, Mom. I'm sorry I don't come home more often."

"It's all right. A mother understands. You're home now."

Kit dismissed the wistful expression on her mother's face and turned her attention to her father. "I'm surprised there's still a mortgage. I would have thought... but don't mind that, how much time do we have? What are the payments? How much is owing on the loan?"

Her dad went silent.

Kit knew his disgruntled look. Michael Wheeler was a private man. He didn't take pleasure in disclosing best practices or personal matters, but for a daughter to help, she might have to yank the nitty-gritty from him.

"Dad, is there something you're not telling me?"

"Stop needling our father, Kit," Samantha hastened to say, sneering. "Don't you see he's upset? Your questions are adding further fuel to a difficult situation. It's just like you to try and manage everything. Let Dad handle this."

"Sam—" Kit appealed, glancing at her sister, "don't get emotional on me. Dad's called us to the ranch for a reason. He needs our help, our support, not more frustration. I can't offer my assistance without further information."

Sam shook her head, not willing to back down. "You can't project manage every hurdle in your life, Kit."

"Children, this is not a time for fighting," Gina Wheeler stated, trying to bring calm. "If we're to survive this ordeal, we must stick together." She rose from the sofa. "I'll put a pot of coffee on. Might dig out the Baileys from last Christmas, too. I don't know about you, but I could use a drink."

Kit watched her mother leave the room. "What did I do?" she asked, raising her hands in supplication. "I'm only trying to hash out this situation. Find a solution. I can't help without knowing how deep we've fallen into the hole. We can't just sit here and drink; we need to communicate, talk for heaven's sake, come up with a plan."

"You're not alone in wanting to make a difference," Cole Wheeler angled, staring her in the face, appearing angry. He clasped his hands in his lap like his father. Kit determined the two men were a lot alike. "You think Sam and I don't want to help? It's not about you, Kit. Let Dad lead the discussion. He brought us here, not you."

Where did her brother's anger come from? She knew that look;

she remembered it from when they were kids. Lies. What information was he keeping from them?

"I'll forgive you for your comment, but since you've discovered your voice, Cole, you've been managing the land, the herd. What can you tell us about the financial difficulty this ranch is facing?"

"Have it your way. The debt extends beyond the mortgage."

"You look so guilty. What have you done?"

"Kit," her father interrupted, staring at the carpeting. "There's credit card debt, too."

"You've got to be kidding. Cole? Have you mismanaged the ranch? This land is our family's legacy, our heritage and our birthright."

"Don't look at me with your high-and-mighty attitude. This house was rotting, the land around it, too before I took over. It required substantial investment. New fences, barn supplies, and I wanted to explore dairy farming, so I invested in milking systems. What other choice did I have? If we're to compete with our neighbors, we have to invest in the future."

"With money we don't have?"

"It's just like you," Samantha scoffed, "to come here in your high heels, your fancy suit, and accuse our brother of mismanaging the ranch."

"Well, hasn't he? We don't own milking cows, Sam. What else is going on here? Facts someone isn't sharing with me?"

"Kids…" Michael Wheeler pleaded, heaving a huge sigh. "Ugly conversations do not help our situation. The ranch is deep in debt. We have to find a solution. Together. This is why I've called you here."

"I'm sorry, Dad. What do you have in mind?" Kit said, wishing her family understood her better, her gut instinct questioning if her father was keeping details of the financial losses secret. And if so, why?

He sighed. "We need to give the bank at least one mortgage payment before the first of the month. Two thousand dollars. That gives us two weeks to find a solution. A plan. We must find a way to satisfy our other creditors, too."

"No!" Dot Wheeler, the family matriarch, spoke up. The room went silent with her outburst and everyone's attention focused on her. "My family will not suffer to keep this ranch. It's worth more than the payments owed. I will sell and give the bank their due."

Kit glanced at her grandmother, observing her pinched expression. The only sign she was angry. She sat on her old pine rocking chair in a family room burdened with memories. She swayed back and forth, her foot tapping against an old worn carpet. Kit had run across the faded roses as a child when it was new, thirty years ago… She wanted her children, if she ever had any, to run across it, too.

"I'm sorry, Gran. This must be hard on you."

Dot stared at something her family couldn't see. "Nice of you to think of me. I've been forgotten in the running of this ranch, and in this conversation, too."

"You've never been forgotten, Mom."

"Son, please hear me out."

"I'll hear whatever you have to say. It's your right. This is your home."

"Michael, Gina, grandchildren," she addressed them all, "this is my home. I've lived here for more than fifty years. Life has not always been easy. I've learned to accept the punches, and to bear the hurt that comes with life. It's time to give in, let go, and move on."

"You don't mean that," Kit began, "this is your home."

"It's four walls holding a gabled roof. Home? A home is a place where the living is cozy and warm, and the kids don't fight. The ranch stopped being a home years ago, when… when John left me too soon. I should never have let go of the reins. I should have kept control of the ranch. It's too late now. I'm tired. I don't want my family to manage this concern, anymore."

"We can help," Samantha said, pleading. "We grew up here. This is our home as much as it is yours. I'm sorry, Gran, about the ranch and more besides."

"It's all right, dear. The decision is made. It's my name on the title, after all."

"We need to talk about this."

"Kit, there's nothing left to discuss," Dot Wheeler proclaimed. "I don't know why your father asked you to come." She stopped rocking, appealing with sadness in her eyes. She stood. "I need to rest. I'm going to my room. I'd like my peace restored when I return."

Kit watched Gran leave. Sadness etched her heart seeing her grandmother's decline, tear-filled eyes, hunched shoulders, her advancing years shadowing the defeat in her eyes. Everyone was silent until they were alone again.

"She doesn't want this?" Kit said, tears filling her eyes. "Gran could not have meant what she said."

"Your grandmother doesn't want her family to face this burden. This is why she wants to sell. She can live comfortably on the proceeds from the sale."

"Dad," Cole appealed, "if we had more time, we could realize the benefits of the investments I've made on the ranch. Kit, Samantha, you have to believe me, I never meant to place the ranch in jeopardy."

"Despite your aggression toward me, I believe you." Kit tried to see her brother's side. "So, what do we do now?"

Gina Wheeler returned to the living room with a coffee pot and five mugs clutched in her hand. "We don't give up. Obstacles might inhibit our progress, but if we work together, we'll find a path forward. Tell me, family, will we pull together?"

"We'll sure as hell try." Samantha took a mug.

"Amen to that." Kit agreed, taking her own mug. "Mom, we might need the Baileys."

"I'll get it," Michael Wheeler offered, rising from his armchair, "after I take a breath of fresh air."

~

KIT FOLLOWED HER FATHER OUTSIDE. The old screen door banged shut and closed behind them.

It was a comforting sound. She'd heard the bang often enough as a child. That and childish laughter as the Wheeler children raced across the threshold. Giggling, laughing like crazy fools. Sam and Cole, sister and brother, chasing her through the doorway in their bare feet. Good memories. Good times. She'd fight to protect them.

She stood beside her father on the portico, staring at Red Angus and Hereford cattle grazing on emerald green pastures that stretched into low-lying hills. White-capped Rocky Mountains glistened beyond. She listened to cattle mooing, studying a landscape so breathtakingly beautiful, her eyes filled with tears, considering they might lose it.

"Dad, I meant what I said. I'd like to help, if I can."

He turned to her, a semblance of a smile on his face. "I wish I had your faith. I admire your strength, your spirit. You never give in, do you? It's not easy managing a ranch. This isn't the first time we've faced a crisis, but this time, we've failed. We've let this old girl down."

"Oh, Dad," Kit said, falling into his arms. "Don't say that. Please, let's not give up without a fight. Surely, there's a plan to make, a strategy to buy us more time. To save the ranch."

"You heard your grandmother, she doesn't want to save the farm."

"I don't believe it. She's lived here for fifty years for a reason. This is her life. Let's go inside. The five of us will come up with a plan."

The screen door opened, and her siblings and mother filed outside. "A beautiful view," her mother said, sipping her coffee. "I thought my grandchildren would see those pastures, play on them, too."

Samantha sat on the porch swing. She was soon swinging, no different than their grandmother had on the rocking chair. "I'd need a boy in my life for that to happen, Mom."

"I didn't mean to detract from our worries."

"We know you want to be a grandmother; you tell us all the time. But back to the subject at hand, I don't think Gran meant what she said."

"How do you know? She appeared determined to me."

"She's a resilient woman, though she's never left the room before."

"True enough," Kit concurred, coming to sit beside her sister. "I don't know what's happened to put this distance between us, but if we work together…"

Sam gazed at her fingernails. "Don't give me that, you left us behind."

Kit studied her sister, her gorgeous strawberry-blonde hair and amber-gold eyes that twinkled with mischief. "I miss you, too, Sam."

Samantha looked at her expression for a long time, soon turning away. The action hurt Kit, but she didn't bring attention to the slight. It would take time to mend this fence. She'd try.

"If you have any ideas," Cole said, "I for one would like to hear them."

"I can cover one mortgage payment, that will buy us more time."

"We could hold an estate sale," Samantha put forward, unsmiling. "Gran says she doesn't want to live here anymore, and if that's true, she won't need fifty years' worth of stuff."

"That's a great idea," Gina added, sipping her coffee. "I can include my artwork in the sale. Some of my friends and colleagues might contribute. Ladies from the church might help, too. When should we have the sale?"

"As soon as possible," Michael said.

"We need time to organize the household effects. We could start tomorrow by inventorying the house, the barn, the surrounding lands. Deciding what we should keep and what we should sell."

"The old attic, too," Michael began, "there's a ton of stuff up there. How long are you home, Kit?"

"I've taken a vacation," Kit said, nibbling at her lip. "Two weeks maybe, but I could press for more time if needed."

"Request three, maybe four." Cole winced, shaking his head. "The old barn is overloaded with pickings, and it could take years to prepare it for a sale. But if we can somehow save the ranch, I'd like to empty it anyway, to use it for the milking operation."

"I'm sorry, Cole, for not having had more faith in you."

"It's okay, big sister."

"I'll start giving some thought to a social media plan," Samantha offered, smacking Kit on the leg.

"Kids, Gina, are you sure you want to do this?"

"Yes." The Wheeler family assented, nodding. Gina toasted them with her cup of coffee.

The chase was on to save the Wheeler Ranch.

CHAPTER 2

*K*it wasn't ready to admit the truth to her family. A vacation? They considered her a professional know-it-all, and she didn't want to disappoint their high opinion by telling them about her failed career, or the fact she didn't have a job.

She was home. Maybe for good.

Cleaning out the old blue barn had been therapeutic, but she was exhausted, every muscle in her body ached and there were still miles to go.

Fifty years of living generated a ton of paraphernalia. Cole had helped her unearth countless objects that could benefit many families, never mind antique or vintage collectors. If she could have afforded assistance from a professional advisor, she'd have hired an estate company to deal with the sorting and pricing of the family goods. Choosing what to sell and what to throw away was guess-work at best, but outside assistance was impossible. The family couldn't afford to lose a dime.

"Kit," her father called, approaching her outside the barn. "I'm impressed with how much you've accomplished. It's been a week since you came home. Look at this barn. It's cleaner than it's been in years."

Standing at the threshold, Kit shook her head, kicking at an imaginary piece of dirt. She was hot, sweaty, and she needed a bath. "Dad, I can't believe how much stuff was crammed inside the barn. Have my parents been holding out on me? Maybe developed a penchant for hoarding?"

"It's not just me," her father laughed, grinning. "Your grandmother loves her dolls, your mother her artwork…"

"What treasures have you been hoarding? Furniture, lamps, old Coca-Cola and Texaco signs…"

"Your mother and grandmother do well enough without me adding to the treasure trove."

"Well, that's funny." Kit giggled, nudging her father on the arm. "Because Cole and I unearthed some Stampede history. That's more your style, isn't it?"

"That's curious. I don't collect vintage items relating to the Stampede. What did you find?"

"An old 1964 poster tucked away in the back of a chuckwagon. According to the poster, Bobby Cortola was playing at the Calgary Stampede that year. Wilf Carter, too."

"It's not mine. The poster could be worth some cash but tell me about the wagon. In all my years of living on this ranch, I don't recall having seen one."

"It was buried in the furthest stall, hidden under an old and rotten tarp."

"A chuckwagon. Are you serious?"

"No… Dad, I made the whole wagon thing up. Seriously, I take after my father, honest to a fault. Right?"

He glanced away. A distance in her father's eyes gave her pause.

"What are you thinking, Dad?"

"Nothing important. I want to see the wagon. Let's go inside."

Kit escorted her father inside the barn. They walked to the farthest stall. Cole had hitched their horse, Molly, to the wagon and pulled it into the center aisle. Old and weathered, the box had seen its time, but it was impressive, all the same.

"I'll be damned. That's a cart all right."

"Come on, Dad, have you been holding out on me? It's been here a long time. I could tell by the layers of dust. How could you live on this land, all your life, and not know it was here?"

Her father stepped closer to the wagon. He drew his fingers across the wood. "Baby blue," he said with a grimace, "just like the color of your eyes. Or at least it must have been when it was new. Maybe Cole's been holding out on us? Maybe this wagon is his?"

"Nope. He was as surprised as me to find it."

"It's a mystery, then. Huh. I'll ask your grandmother, see if we can learn the truth. If there's a story to tell, she's sure to know it. I'll ask her; maybe at dinner tonight."

Kit followed her father to the entrance of the barn. "You know, Kit, there's a lot of antique dealers who love this type of stuff. The cart, the Stampede poster, the signs; they could be worth a lot of money. How will we determine each item's worth? Maybe we should have hired the estate company."

"They'd want their cut. We need the funds from the sale. Cole and Sam have been doing their best to get prices through the Internet. It's not a perfect system, but hopefully, we're close to assessing the true value of each item."

"Speaking of your siblings, where are they?"

"Cole went to check on the herd. It's calving season and a cow he's been watching is missing. Samantha is rummaging through the attic. I almost feel guilty about sending her there." Kit snickered into her hand. "You know, because of the dust. She's been up there a long time. I should see what's keeping her."

"Kit. The tricks you kids continue to play on each other. They need to stop. You're adults now. I knew there was skullduggery going on when you were young, but I won't get involved with more serious behaviors now."

"We're fine, Dad. No need to lecture."

"Kit—"

"Look, we need to overcome the burdens of the past. I promise you, we're trying. We're working on it."

"Okay. Before I go, what can I do to help?"

"Speak to Mom. She's in the kitchen washing china sets, crystal bowls, vases and the like that Gran wants to put in the sale."

"I guess your mother wants to keep the ranch, then."

"Of course she does. I was about to tell you that I've emptied an old cabinet. Mom wants to place novelty items inside. Gran has committed a few of her dolls."

Her dad smiled at her. "That's surprising. I thought you might need some help with heavy lifting, but Cole and you have achieved a lot on your own."

"There are old tools, signs and furnishings to sort through. Maybe you could help Cole with pricing the items for sale. Tomorrow maybe? Especially if, as Cole suspects, the cow is calving."

"I'll find Cole and see about the cow in case he needs any help. I'm letting him decide what we keep, what we discard, what we sell, too."

"Stands to reason."

Kit wiped her hands on her jeans. "I'll accompany you to the house, see what's keeping Sam."

KIT CLIMBED THE LADDER, stepping carefully on each rung, and soon pulling herself through a rectangular opening in the ceiling. Standing on the edge, she wrinkled her nose, smelling dust and memories long forgotten. Dust. She was sick of dirt and grime. She groaned, not knowing where to step. Boxes were stacked willy-nilly, cluttering up the tiny space.

Poor Sam. Guilt assailed Kit for assigning this task. Where did one start?

"Samantha?" she called, heaving a sigh. "Where are you?"

She stepped gingerly forward, negotiating each step, shifting boxes aside with her knee, the old floor creaking beneath her weight. "Over here," her sister replied, sneezing. "Be careful, there's a lot of obstacles. As you can see, the boxes were not placed in an organized way."

"Oh, Sam. How will we manage all of this, this stuff?" Kit groaned, rubbing her nose, shaking her head, raising her hands in appeal. "There are boxes stacked everywhere."

"I wondered when you would come searching for me." She sneezed. "We would have loved this castle keep when we were kids. Then, we'd have made a fortress inside the mess. You won't believe the history I've found. The clothing we could have worn. Come on over, if you dare."

She shuffled closer to where Sam sat on the floor. "What have you found?"

Sam giggled. "Old fur coats, farm dresses, vintage hats and gloves. They must have been our grandmother's. I can't imagine selling them."

Kit sat on a cardboard box, but it gave way, crumpling inward. Samantha giggled when she fell backwards. "I'm sorry, Kit," she laughed, reaching for her hand. "I should have warned you about the obstacles. Come, take my hand."

Kit accepted Sam's grasp. "I guess I have no choice but to sit on the floor."

"I know there's dirt, but it won't hurt you, princess."

"I'm far from royalty." Kit sat on the floor beside her sister. "I come from good farm stock. Honey, believe it or not, I can manage a bit of dirt."

Sam didn't respond for a minute.

"When will you tell Dad about your job?"

"What about it?"

"That you're not on vacation, like you told him."

Kit glanced downward, looking away from her sister. "I don't know what you're talking about."

"You might as well admit it," Sam said, scrutinizing her expression. "You don't have a job. You have a permanent vacation."

"Okay, so I admit it. I don't have a job. I was laid off. How did you find out?"

"Social media."

"My professional life has not been shared on any platforms."

"True enough." Sam grasped her hand. "It's been my rule not to share other people's downfalls, it's a matter of courtesy, but one of your friends has a big mouth."

"Stacey, am I right?"

"She was only too happy to see you released. Bitch. Hey look, I'm sorry you lost your job, if you must know. I thought we could talk about it."

"That comes as a surprise since we don't talk about our personal lives much. In fact, we hardly talk at all."

"We could change. If you were not so…"

"Stubborn? Oh Sam—" Kit shook her head. "We'd have far fewer problems if we were not so much alike. But tell me, have you told the family?"

"Nah. It's not my place to share your secrets. I figure when you're ready, you'll tell them yourself."

"Thanks for talking to me first. I should have told you. I don't know why I didn't."

Sam released her hand. "You're not a failure. You'll find another opportunity. I'm sorry you lost your job, but I'm happy you're home. Despite what I told you the other day, you're the right project manager to lead our family out of this nightmare, to save the ranch."

"Thank you for your confidence in me."

"You're welcome. Now, enough sorrow. Want to know what I unearthed from this archeological dig?"

"I'm dying to know," Kit blurted, laughing so hard her belly ached. "Tell me."

"A stash of photos stored inside an old suitcase. They're amazing."

"Oh yeah, pass the case over."

Kit accepted the suitcase into her hands and placed it on the floor in front of her. She grasped the metal fastenings with her thumbs, sliding each until the latches sprang upward. She lifted the lid. Piles of letters, photos, and other memorabilia were stored in neat piles, tied with baby-blue ribbons. She grabbed a stack from the top, untied the trimming, and began leafing through the photos.

"Will you look at this?" she said, studying an aged portrait of her grandmother. "Gran is beautiful. Curly dark hair tucked beneath a vintage hat and an old pencil skirt set off with a white belt. What a beauty."

"There's one where she's holding a rifle at the fair. Her face is alight with humor, even though she looks like she's ready to shoot someone."

"Gran has always had a zest for life, if you know what I mean." Kit smirked, placing the photo at the back of the stack.

"Did you see this one, a photo with a young man in front of the farmhouse? This must be our grandfather, John Wheeler."

Sam reached forward, and Kit passed the photo into her hands. "I'm sure you're right. I can see the family resemblance to our father. It's remarkable. Gran doesn't have many photos of him in the house. Strange she'd keep them here. Let's take them downstairs. Surprise her."

"Look at this," Kit exclaimed, feeling like she'd unearthed a buried treasure. "The chuckwagon we found in the barn. John Wheeler is sitting on the driver's seat."

Sam glanced at the photo. "He has a big smile on his face. Looks like he's enjoying sitting on the seat."

"What happened to him, Kit?"

"Passed away after a farming accident. I recall Mom saying he fell from a tractor, hitting his head."

16

"How sad," Sam replied, passing the photo back.

Kit placed the photos back inside the suitcase and then tied them with the faded blue ribbon. She grasped a stack of envelopes. "Do you think these could be love letters?"

"We should leave well enough alone. Private correspondence between our grandparents. We shouldn't read them. Right?"

"Come on, Sam. Aren't you the least bit curious about what's inside? Once we turn this suitcase over to our grandmother…"

"She might not let us see them again. The way the contents were buried inside this hoard? Okay, we'll only read one letter."

"Okay." Kit giggled, enjoying the sudden camaraderie between sisters while untying the ribbon and unfolding the parchment. "We'll keep it to ourselves. We won't tell anyone. I'll read it to you…"

June 1964. My darling Dot,

I miss you! I've just finished competing at Guy Weadick days in High River. Baby Blue came in with a good time. The team didn't win, but we're excited about the next competition at Wainwright, followed by the Ponoka Stampede on the first of July.

I know I promised we would return home before the Calgary Stampede, but Dot, we're hot on a win and the boys are itching for the next race. Now darling, I know how you feel about this sport. You've nattered at me often enough about spending more time at home. I understand your concerns about the half mile, as well as your husband being gone all summer. Risking your anger, I must take this gamble. We need to secure a win to purchase more horses, more cows, and a pretty dress for my blue-eyed beauty. Think of how the purse could benefit the farm, our lives, and the child soon to be born?

I'll be home soon, honey. Wait for me. If you have the presence of mind, pray for a win!

Yours truly, John Wheeler.

"Grandfather Wheeler was a chuckwagon driver?" Sam said with surprise. "Did you know about this family history?"

Kit still held the letter, but her hand relaxed to her lap. "Huh, imagine that. No. I didn't. He passed away before our father was born. Dad doesn't know much about his father, or his family history for that matter. A chuckwagon driver, wow, that's interesting."

"When was Dad born?"

"I'm not sure and it's terrible I don't know the date, but according to grandfather's letter, our grandmother was pregnant in June of 1964."

"Given the information, our father must have been born on August 3, 1964."

"Grandfather Wheeler passed away prior to his son's birth. I know this for sure. And grandfather was competing, taking to the Stampede circuit. How many races happen over the summer?"

"I have no idea."

"Sam, I have a sneaking suspicion something's not right here. A wagon buried in the barn and a tan leather suitcase hidden in the attic. Why?"

"Kit, I see the wheels turning in your brain. Don't envision stories where none exist. This isn't a Nancy Drew mystery for heaven's sake. And to be fair, there's a lot of stuff cluttering up this attic." Sam coughed, rising to a standing position. "But learning our grandfather drove the chucks, now that's interesting. I'd like to hear the story. We should find out. We should ask Gran at dinner."

"Do you think it might upset her?"

"Why would it upset her? It's her past."

"Well, you know how it is, some people don't like to be reminded of the past."

"Don't you want to know the truth?"

"Yes, of course I do," Kit said. Her gut told her there was a story buried here, and once she had a seed of a mystery, she was like a dog to a bone, she had to chew out the truth.

"You ask, okay?"

"Me? Samantha, you treat me as if I'm a pariah coming home, and then you think you'll take it upon yourself to push me toward the truth."

"Why are you so afraid? I see it in your eyes."

"You know Gran when she gets excited," Sam elaborated.

Kit glanced at the memories, bearing in mind the turmoil one letter could cause. Her forehead wrinkled with concern as she questioned if she should raise the subject of the suitcase and the contents inside. But what could it hurt? Might be fun to share the memorabilia with the family. Photos and letters should be protected, anyway.

She refolded the letter and placed it with the others, then wrapped the blue ribbon around the stack, placing the package back inside the suitcase.

"I'm exhausted," Kit said, closing the case. "Let's go down."

"Are you bringing the suitcase with you?" Sam asked, raising her eyes.

"Yes, I am. Doesn't hurt to have a prop when you're about to say hello to history."

THE WHEELERS HAD GATHERED TOGETHER at the dinner table. Gina had cooked a roast beef, mashed potatoes, and too-soft carrots. Conversation was lacking as everyone was tired from their labors. They ate in silence. Kit took a deep breath. No time like the present to pose her question.

"We've been slugging through a lot of paraphernalia while preparing the ranch for the sale. We've found a lot of treasures. That part of the work has been fun." Kit smiled, glancing at Sam. "I was surprised to learn Grandfather Wheeler was a chuckwagon driver."

Her grandmother's eyes widened, she took a deep breath, then resumed eating her meal as if Kit hadn't disclosed anything.

"Not to my knowledge," Michael Wheeler offered, grasping his water glass. "But there is a wagon in the barn. Mom, speaking about the wagon, can you tell us about it?"

Gran took a deep breath. She gazed at her plate. Kit saw the way her right hand clutched the knife. "So, you've found a wagon in the barn. That shouldn't come as a surprise on a working ranch."

"It's interesting," Michael pointed out, "what do you know about it?"

Granny nodded her head, her expression strained. "It's not uncommon. John used it when he was haying."

Kit took a deep breath. Oh dear, it was worse than she thought. "Did Grandfather use it for more than work around the ranch? Samantha and I found a vintage suitcase in the attic. It contained photographs of a young man, a wagon, and, we thought the man might have been…"

Gran dropped the knife, sat taller in the chair and took a deep breath. "Who gave you permission to poke around my belongings, without my consent?"

"There wasn't a name on the suitcase to my knowledge," Sam said with a grimace, staring at Kit.

Gran's face turned as red as the carnations in the center of the table. Kit saw her grandmother was trying to maintain her composure. She didn't get angry often, but her pert little lips couldn't conceal her displeasure.

"We've been sorting through the belongings for the sale, you know that, Gran. We certainly didn't mean to…"

"I told you. We're selling this place. There's no need…"

"Yes, but if we do decide to follow through with selling the ranch, we need to sort through the belongings. Decide what's important to you. You know, Gran. What to keep, what to sell, and what to discard."

"Regardless the reason, managing an estate sale does not excuse you from snooping through my belongings. It's my life history. It doesn't belong to you."

Michael Wheeler sat taller. "Mom, calm yourself. Why are you so upset? So, the girls found old photos inside a suitcase. What's the big deal? In fact, where is this suitcase? I have not seen many photos of my father and I'd like to."

"No!" Gran replied, her face turning scarlet. She banged her fist on the table. The plate and the cutlery jumped.

"We should drop this discussion," Gina Wheeler advised, "you're upsetting Dot."

"Where is the suitcase?" Dorothy Wheeler stated, rising from her chair, hands on her hips.

"It's in my room, Gran," Kit indicated, placing her fork on her plate. "I'll go get it for you."

"No. I'll come with you."

Michael pushed his chair back from the table. He too seemed angry now. Kit felt guilty for what she had done and didn't know how to proceed now.

"I'll accompany both of you. I have a right to know my father. Mom, why are you so upset?"

"Dad, Gran, I didn't know finding the suitcase would cause so much trouble, but perhaps it's best that Gran and I go see the suitcase together. What do you think?"

Her grandmother sat on the dining chair, then placed her old wrinkled hands against her face and began to cry. "I never wanted you to know."

Kit rose from the table and went to her grandmother's side, placing her hand on her shoulder. "Oh Gran, whatever mystery you've kept, maybe it's time to share it with your family."

"Maybe you're right, Kit."

She shook her head, wiped at the tears spilling from her eyes.

"Let's adjourn to the living room. Kit, go get the suitcase."

"Are you sure, Gran?"

"I'm sure."

⁓

Kɪᴛ ᴡᴀᴛᴄʜᴇᴅ the sentiment wrinkle her grandmother's expression. The tan vintage suitcase rested against the ottoman. She studied it carefully; her fingers slid against the leather grain as if the past had come to life beneath her fingertips, and the contents important.

"I have not touched this case for over fifty-three years. Not since after John passed away."

"You don't have to do this, Mom," Michael Wheeler offered. "I can see how hard this is on you."

She grasped the locking mechanism, massaging her thumb across the metal, soon releasing the clasp.

"It's okay, son. I felt it was important to protect my family from the truth, but I've lived my life as an honest woman, and the past has found a way to be revealed."

She glanced at Kit meaningfully, making her feel guilty for her part, then opened the lid. "John was a thoughtful man. No matter how far he travelled, he found the time to write."

No longer angry, Gran looked pensive, sad as she reminisced, reaching for a stack of old parchment. "I didn't see him much in the summer months, you see. He was always hungry for the next race. Leaving the farm work to me, and a few able-bodied men. He travelled from town to town, venturing across Alberta, taking Baby Blue with him."

"Baby Blue?" Kit appealed.

She smiled, but the light didn't reach her eyes. She appeared as if she might cry. Again.

"He named the wagon after me," Gran disclosed, sharing her melancholy, her eyes wet. "The color of my eyes."

Kit shook her head, took her hand to her mouth. "Gran, I'm so sorry."

"No, darling," she whispered, wiping a tear from her cheek. "It's time the truth was known."

She placed the letters inside the suitcase and grasped a stack of photographs. She gingerly untied the ribbon and gazed at the images. She scrutinized one particular photograph, then showed it to everyone assembled in the room.

"This is an image of your father, Michael. My John, he was handsome, don't you think?"

Michael reached for the photo and Grandmother let her son hold it. "So here he is, standing beside the wagon."

"You look like your father."

"So, what's the mystery, Mom? Why was it so important for you to hide this suitcase in the attic?"

She leaned backward in the armchair and went to a place Kit couldn't see. "I remember the day as if it were yesterday. I was washing dishes in the sink when the phone rang. I grabbed a dish towel and dried my hands. Picked up the receiver. Said hello into the line…"

"Dot?"

"Bennet, is that you?"

"Yes, it's me, Dot."

"You don't sound like yourself. Is something wrong?"

"There's been an accident…"

"I dropped the phone."

Kit rushed to her grandmother's side and knelt beside her. She could see how pale her grandmother had become and she was fearful for her. She wished they had never found the suitcase. "You don't need to say anymore, Gran."

"He loved to race, my John. It gave him pleasure. The smell of the horses, the reins clutched in his hands, the wind as it puffed through his hair." She heaved a sigh, staring at the suitcase. "He said he was coming home soon. He never arrived."

"What happened?" Michael asked. "You might as well tell us."

Gran turned to her son. "John was determined to pull in a good time. Bennet told me they were close to winning at High River. He came around the corner too fast and the wagon lifted. He slipped from the driver's seat, falling..."

"I know this happened a long time ago," Kit remarked, "I'm sorry, sorry for your pain."

She nodded. "It was a long time ago."

"Wow," Gina chipped in, "that's a sad and heartbreaking story."

"So," Cole added, "we come from a strong heritage. Cows, horses, and wagons. What happened to the horses?"

"I sold them. I didn't want past-markers lying around that could harm my son. In many families, chuckwagon racing is a tradition shared between the generations. I had to end it. Michael was due in a month and I didn't want him to meet the same fate."

"If you had discarded Baby Blue, or the memorabilia, we would never have learned the truth. Why did you keep it all?"

"Michael, your father loved the wagon. I wanted to haul it away. I wanted to burn it in the most amazing bonfire this ranch had ever seen, but the wagon was all I had left. A remembrance. A keepsake from a time we shared. I couldn't do it. So, I hid it away instead. Bennet helped me."

"He was a friend of Dad's. That's how your friendship began?"

"Bennet's a former outrider, he was part of John's team. A good friend of mine, too."

"This is it," Sam dared to say, rising from the sofa. "This story is sad, but amazing, too. We need to share the wagon with the world. It could be the story to save the ranch."

"What did you say?" Dorothy asked.

"To save the ranch, we need a stronger approach than a sale. We need an idea that will generate sympathy and excitement with the people. A concept that will grab the public's attention and have them yearning to help us. If I share the Wheeler's family history— You know, what happened to John Wheeler and the ranch's subsequent devastation? The media attention could have people congregating at the sale."

"I don't think that's what Gran had in mind," Kit chided, but she agreed that Sam had raised a valid point.

Cole tapped his fingers against his denim jeans. "We need a slogan. Something strong."

"Baby Blue rides again," her dad said, pondering.

"No! I won't have it."

"It was an accident, Mom. We should take the gamble."

Gran stood. Kit had never seen her so angry, or so stern. "What do you think you're going to do? Take the wagon back to the track? I won't have it. I should have burned the cart when I had the chance."

"Calm down, that's not what I'm suggesting."

But now the idea was on the table.

"Not such a bad plan," Cole teased.

"Baby Blue rides again?" Sam questioned, mulling the idea. "We have to do it. One more ride; we don't have to win."

"No!" Gran bellowed, shaking her head. "I won't let you."

"Mom, did you ever sit on Baby Blue? Go for a ride?"

"Yes, of course I did."

"You're our family matriarch. When the picture is taken, you have to be the one sitting on the wagon. And the rest of us, we'll stand by your side."

"I can't do it."

Her father appeared excited. A new light shone in his eyes. "Sometimes we have to take a risk. You know that I'm a gambler and I'm not afraid to place a bet on this family."

"Michael Wheeler, I won't protect you any longer. You're part of the reason this ranch is in trouble. Don't contribute further to bad ideas."

"What?" Kit exclaimed, shocked to hear the disclosure. "What is Gran talking about?"

"It's true. I have a gambling problem. I won't deny it."

"I wanted to tell you," Cole admitted, shaking his head. "Dad has gamed a lot of funds away from this ranch."

"Does he have access to the financial accounts?"

"I'm right here in the room, Kit. You can ask me."

"Well, do you?"

He appeared sheepish.

"No. Cole has had me removed from the accounts. This is why he has retained management of the ranch while I try to get my act together."

Kit gazed at her brother. "I'm sorry, Cole. I should have had more faith in you."

"Apology accepted. We've got this, Sis. We're going to be okay."

"Let's get back to Baby Blue." Sam appealed to her family. "We must consider our roles, like who'll drive and who'll be an outrider?"

"I can drive," Cole offered, smiling.

"I guess that leaves the sisters to be your outriders." Kit giggled, excited about the adventure to come.

"You know this is not a joke, right?" their grandmother added. "Chuckwagon racing is a dangerous sport."

"We understand that," Kit exclaimed, agreeing. "We know what happened to Grandpa John. Did he ever win?"

"He came close."

"We do this for him," Michael said, "and in his name. We don't need to win the race, we just need to save the Wheeler Ranch."

Dot Wheeler slammed the suitcase shut. "Over my dead body. If you think I'll let you do this without a fight, you don't know me very well."

Kit watched her grandmother get up and leave the room, carrying the suitcase in her hand. She'd never witnessed such emotion. "Do we go against our own grandmother?"

"If we do this, we have to be committed as a family. Are we?" Michael Wheeler asked.

"Yes!" they declared unanimously.

In the end, Dot Wheeler had refused to sit on the bench seat of

Baby Blue, so Kit had been forced to expose her inner self. Sam had snapped a photo of her with the chuckwagon in the background.

Sam had commiserated that a picture could be worth a thousand shares if the emotion was captured in the right light. Kit didn't care for the final image. She appeared too thoughtful, too pale. A hopeless woman standing on the prairie with the pond in the background, sensationalizing a historic story.

Sam thought her look was perfect. Kit didn't understand why.

The sun was setting behind her and it seemed like a family's life was setting, too. Kit couldn't see any good coming from this photo.

CHAPTER 3

A cup of coffee in one hand and a newspaper in the other, Gabe Bradshaw scrutinized the headline in the morning paper while waiting for his team to assemble in the boardroom. 'Baby Blue to ride again.' The journalistic account held local appeal, the type of intrigue that captured public attention and won a reader's sympathy, too. Whose heart wouldn't bleed for a family in trouble?

He scrutinized the photo, seeing how the photographer had captured the emotion on Kit Wheeler's face. The sadness seemed to underscore her baby-blue eyes. Kit Wheeler, standing like a ghost from the past with a wagon in the background. He was drawn to her rugged beauty, and her determination to try.

The Wheeler family had an intriguing history. An oil company could benefit from the media attention. Did he want to go that far? Yes, he did, and he would.

"Good morning, Gabe," Mitchell said as he strolled into the boardroom. "Your mother and I missed you at dinner last night. How was your weekend?"

"Oh, you know, Friday night at the gym, Saturday, dinner and a movie."

"Lindsey?"

"Lindsey," Gabe verbalized, shaking his head, "is a colleague of mine. I don't mix business with pleasure. I take after, well, my father."

"Then who? Don't tell me you went alone."

"Is it a crime to go to a movie alone?"

Just then, Jared Wang, the public relations officer entered the boardroom, followed soon after by the company's media and technology expert, Lindsey. She was beautiful, big brown eyes and long dark hair with blonde strands painted at the ends. They were friends. He wouldn't cross the lines of propriety or respect, even if at times he sensed she might want him to. Both officers took a seat.

"Good morning." Hope groaned, joining those already assembled, carrying a Starbucks mug.

"Kids keep you up last night?" Mitchell asked, appearing concerned.

She reached for a boardroom chair and sat across from their father. "It's days like this I wish I wasn't your vice president, Dad. Tiffany's fighting a cold; I should be at home. She couldn't attend preschool this morning, being ill, so Mom's taking care of her. James is at daycare, so far, he's not sick."

"Sorry to hear my niece is unwell, Hope, but now that we're assembled, has anyone seen the headlines in the morning paper?" Gabe Bradshaw pushed two newspapers to the center of the boardroom table. "I've called you together to talk about an article on the front page."

"I might have seen a posting on Facebook," Lindsey said, reaching for a paper.

"Not me," Jared offered, grasping the extra paper. "I took the weekend off social media. Not so much as one tweet."

Gabe placed his mug and paper on the boardroom table, then took a seat at the head. He had a lot to prove since accepting the presidential seat recently vacated by his father. He aimed to make his father proud, but he'd inherited a lot of pressure along with the position and his father hadn't exactly vacated the company, still insisting on attending all meetings of the board.

"Let me tell you, I have not been able to keep my thoughts from this story since it broke over the weekend on social media. The Wheeler family has captured media attention. From Longview, Alberta, they were once a prominent family in the Stampede circuit. Has anyone heard of the Wheeler family or their Stampede history?"

"No," Jared replied, glancing at the image of the matriarch's granddaughter. "Just look at this powerful photo. Whoever shot the picture captured an intensity of emotion. What a stunner with her blue eyes."

"Pretty in an austere kind of way," Lindsey said with a grimace, "but I don't think you called us together to talk about the woman's facial features."

"True. I want to discuss our brand and how the company might benefit from the Wheeler story."

"What do you have in mind?" Mitchell Bradshaw asked, not appearing overly impressed.

"I want to make contact with the family, perhaps offer sponsorship of some sort. Attaching our brand to their name could put us in a more positive light, to show our adversaries we are a good company, a brand our clients and customers can trust."

"How exactly does aligning our brand with a downtrodden family help us?" Mitchell appealed, pointing at the paper. "Sympathy does not promote TarSan Oil as far as I'm concerned."

"I see what you're suggesting, Gabe," Hope offered, picking up the paper from the table. "From what I observed from the article, the Wheeler grandchildren, particularly one Kit Wheeler, want to revisit their grandfather's legacy by winning a chuckwagon race, an event that took his life. Brave family. Brave woman. But she can't possibly succeed without financial support."

"Yes, Hope, but how does offering our financial support benefit TarSan Oil?"

"Many have taken the view that our company does not impact environmental issues in a positive way," Jared offered, tapping a pen on a pad of paper. "One could argue this situation is the perfect opportunity for sad-advertising."

"Sad what?" Mitchell asked.

"It's a clever marketing tool," Lindsey explained. "A sad situation presents an opportunity for marketing and a company responds in an over-the-top way, warming the hearts of everyone watching the news. The feed. Whatever… People connect to this type of brand marketing, they eat this stuff up."

"Okay, sure. But wouldn't we be better fostering new partnerships and cleaning up the environmental damage we've caused."

"We can do that, we have been doing that," Jared exclaimed, thoughtfully. "I for one like the public relations opportunity we might gain from this story. Gabe is right, but we have to move fast."

Gabe sipped his coffee. "What opportunities do you see? How might an 'over-the-top' contribution help?"

"Their ranch is in jeopardy, they need money to save it."

"We can't hand them a blank check to save their ranch," Mitchell Bradshaw challenged.

Gabe took a deep breath. It wasn't easy being the president of TarSan Oil. His father had given him the keys to his office, so to speak, but he wouldn't vacate the presidential chair. It was frustrating. And then his father wondered why he avoided coming home for Sunday dinner.

"That's not what I'm suggesting. I want a commitment in return."

Lindsey gazed at her phone, thumbing through a newly created Facebook page for the Wheeler family.

"There's an estate sale this weekend. Frankly, it looks like a county fair taking place, and many people have commented they're attending. Gabe, the siblings are being auctioned off to the highest bidder for the chance of a date."

"Really?" Gabe said, not able to hide his interest.

"If I support this idea, the president needs to attend the estate sale." Mitchell expressed his amusement. "Gabe, I know we're in the company of your colleagues, but if I agree to this, ah, sad-advertising campaign, I want you to win the date with Miss Austere."

Gabe glanced at the paper. There was a quality in this woman's posture, a strength that drew his attention to her. He could see the struggle in her baby-blue eyes.

"I'll do it. I'll make the bid for Kit Wheeler. It's the perfect opportunity to plead our case."

"Should I place a bid on Samantha?" Jared asked.

"I don't expect you to place a bid, but if you're game, the company will pay the fee. Can't hurt to align ourselves with two members of the Wheeler family. I don't mind saying, Jared Wang, the two of you have job roles in common. Samantha Wheeler is a social media wizard. You could learn from her expertise."

"I'm game."

"What about you, Dad? Will you join us at the ranch on Saturday?"

"You know how I roll, son. When a statement needs to be made, it's made strongest when a family sticks together. If Tiffany's feeling better, she'd love to see the ranch. Pet a horse, stroke a cow? Could be a photo opportunity for our family."

"You're welcome to take them," Hope said, sighing. "Given the way I'm feeling, I'll probably be sick in bed."

"What do you think, team? Are we in this together?"

"Yes."

"What about Cole Wheeler?" Lindsey asked. "Would you mind, Gabe, if I bet on him?"

"I don't know. Such an action could be seen as dominating the auction. We don't want to be seen as over-reaching."

Lindsey smiled, lowering her gaze. Gabe could see what she wanted, but he wasn't interested no matter how much his father pressured, or his mother suggested. He'd find a woman, a wife, when the time was right.

"See how you feel on the day. It'll be your choice. Same offer as Jared."

"Hmm," she muttered, appearing sad. Gabe didn't want to hurt her, so he had to be honest.

"Does anyone have other matters to contribute to this meeting?"

Gabe glanced at his team members. He trusted them. Jared jotted on his notepad, Lindsey shook her head. Hope sighed, and his father smirked. He had a lot to prove to his father.

"All right, team, we'll call this meeting to a close. It's an hour drive to Longview, I propose we travel together."

"Patti and I will travel together, accompanied by our grandchildren. If they're well enough to go, that is."

"I'm sorry." Hope wiped her forehead. "I'll have to sit this one out."

"This leaves Lindsey and Jared. Would you like a ride?"

"Road trip," Jared interjected, smiling. "I'll get the coffee for the ride."

"I'm in," Lindsey said, appearing hopeful. "But I'm claiming shotgun."

Jared rose from his chair but paused at the doorway. "I'll do some historical research on the family. I'll give you a full report on Friday."

"Keep this quiet. No posts on social media. I don't want our competitors getting wind of this idea."

"I'm going home to bed. Too tired to look at Facebook."

"Rest easy, little sister."

"I'll pick up James from his daycare."

"Thanks, Dad."

Gabe soon found himself alone in the boardroom. He picked up the paper from the table and studied the image of Kit Wheeler. What attracted him to her story? He wasn't usually so drawn to an issue, despite how he had expressed himself to the team. He honestly wanted to help this family, if he could, and he wanted to speak to one Kit Wheeler.

Austere? He didn't think so. He dropped the newspaper in the recycle bin and left the boardroom but paused when he reached the entrance to his office. One beauty inside the paper caused him to rethink the blue bin. He retraced his steps, returned to the boardroom and retrieved the paper.

This story was one that couldn't be thrown away.

He tucked the paper beneath his arm and resumed his business day.

CHAPTER 4

Sam had prepared an extensive listing for the estate sale. Kit was impressed, not only with the detail but also with the many supporters who had come forward to assist their family. The sheer numbers of people were surprising. Some of the names on the list, compelling.

Local artists had contributed their paintings, time and talent, having transformed inexpensive furniture pieces into wondrous works of art. A local singer had offered her vocal services, insisting her stage become none other than the wagon, Baby Blue. One artist, keener than the rest, had put his mark on the wagon, refurbishing the cart to its original color of baby blue.

Mom's church congregation had offered to oversee the event and had gifted items to include in the silent auction. The kitchen volunteers had supported the cause by offering to bake and then sell cakes and cookies, coffee, tea, and hot chocolate, too. The attention had become overwhelming. Kit didn't know if her grandmother wanted to laugh or cry.

"I know that look, Kit Wheeler. You've seen a problem on your *lengthy* list that meets with your disapproval."

"Well," Kit sighed, glancing at Sam. "One particular item gives me pause."

"The date night, right?"

"A night out with a stranger? Sam— This is happening too fast. I admit it. Your social media skills at getting the word out have been nothing short of amazing, but the circumstances we find ourselves in, well, this is the start of a media circus." Kit pulled the draperies aside and glanced beyond the window frame. "The cameras are waiting, hoping for another update, another interview. It's a lie. Someone is bound to learn the truth."

"They're hungry," Sam remarked, standing near her sister's side. "Those cameras and the reporters in front of them are our medium. We have to play them."

"I feel like we're using people. I want to save the ranch, but is this the right way to achieve our objective?"

"You're uncomfortable because the story is challenging our personal boundaries, but intrigue draws attention, when the public realizes the suffering is real. Look, we're trying to create a partnership, a tribe if you will. One who will support us as we move forward with our goals."

"Our goals? Cole will have to drive the wagon. I'm having second thoughts about racing Baby Blue. It's upsetting our grandmother. We're forcing her to relive her husband's death. It's not fair."

"Kit, you have to listen to me. Without the race, there's no story, and therefore no money. We have to go the distance, the half mile if you will."

Sam persisted, scrutinizing her face. She stepped closer and grasped Kit's arm. "I don't think I've ever witnessed such fear in you. I know there's a lot to take in," Sam said, pointing at the checklist, "but we can do this."

Kit swallowed, perusing her sister's steadfast expression. She wouldn't object to the workload, or the measures they had achieved together, because finally, they were sisters working toward a common goal.

"Even the date night?"

"Especially the date. It's my favorite part of the planning." Sam laughed, urging her to the door.

"Ah," Kit sighed, wincing. "Sam, this better be a good date, because…"

"Because nothing, darling. We've got this!"

"I hope so. Are you ready to go outside and face the media circus?"

"I've always been ready, but Kit?" Sam asked, gazing at her meaningfully.

"Yes?"

"Let me do the talking. You put the coral lipstick on I gave you, brush your cheeks with color and appear Western. Sashay, sway like you're a two-stepping filly on her way to a barn raising or a sweetheart's dance. Be the woman a boy might take home to his mama."

"Sam…"

"Kit," Sam appealed, amusement lighting her expression. "Your dinner date could be watching. You know what Mom's hoping for with this date, right?"

Kit groaned. "I can manage the performance, but these jeans are too tight. I can barely breathe."

"You best get used to them. No more skirts and high heels, well, unless they're made of denim and short. You're a Wheeler, a wrangler, look the part."

"Okay. You're enjoying this way too much! Let's get this show over with."

CHAPTER 5

*G*abe exited his BMW X1. He wouldn't usually park in a field filled with a variety of vehicles over his concern of negligent car owners who might dent his doors, but today, he looked beyond scratched silver paint. He stood on the floorboard of his vehicle, taking in an incredible mountain view. Oh man, without the congestion, one might hear the chirping of birdsong and be able to breathe clean mountain air. Instead, the wail of a country singer infused the air, wafting to him from afar.

"Look at these cars," Jared exclaimed, surprise etching his facial features. "It seems like the family saga has taken on a new life. I wasn't sure the media exposure would engage the Wheeler audience this way. Look at the conversions. The family must be impressed."

"Look's good, doesn't it, when you speak of a family's troubles in terms of social media attention."

"Hey, I don't deny the story is a sad one. I'm not insensitive to their downfall. But that's why we're here, right? To convert their tribe to our base?"

Gabe stepped from the floorboard to a pasture trampled with tire tracks. He shut the door, watching as a family of four rushed past.

"It was my idea, Jared."

"Does it matter whose idea it was? I've worked with you for over five years. The only time I've seen a look of consternation on your face is when you're thinking of your father."

"You're perceptive. I'm trying to prove my worth. Trying to take his previous business initiatives in a new direction."

"Well, you're the president, right? Isn't it your job?"

Gabe glanced at his public relations expert, seeing his enthusiasm. He chuckled. "President with a babysitter more like. I don't know why I'm giving you insights into the company narrative. My father would never confide his innermost secrets."

"We have more than an employer-employee relationship, and I know you value my opinion."

"Okay, since you know so much, tell me why Lindsey didn't show up for work today, pleading a headache instead?"

Jared glanced backward momentarily, walking between an old brown car and a black Ford truck, but his look seemed perceptive. "Are you pressing for the truth?"

"I might already know, but why don't you inform me. You have a friendship with Lindsey. Let me know we're in sync with our ideas."

"It's simple, my friend. The only man she's shopping for has the last name Bradshaw, not Wheeler. She has a thing for you."

Gabe sighed, shaking his head. "I'm not interested. I should let her down easy and terminate her employment. This business relationship has become too complicated."

"But you won't do that."

"Why not?"

Jared smirked, side-stepping a kid who ran in front of him. "Because she's awesome at her job."

"Why does life have to be so complicated? What do you recommend, then?"

"Find her a better option. A man who will return her feelings, or better yet, a woman who will return yours."

"Fat chance of me being a matchmaker." Gabe laughed, striding alongside Jared in a stream of people. "How many cars do you think are parked in this lot?"

"I've already calculated the engagements. At least one hundred, and I see in the distance a Global News van, CTV and CBC cameras. It's good you wore your best suit jacket. You'll want to stand out in the crowd."

"Yeah, and the new Wranglers might make an impression, too. Business fashion with a Western edge. Perfect for the occasion. Probably a complete waste though, I'm only the son of Mitchell Bradshaw and most people know who I am anyway."

"Well, just in case you're approached, you must appreciate what the family is suffering and how TarSan Oil means to help."

"You've got it all planned."

"Gabe, do you want to give a meaningful impression, an action that might promote the family's interests and get our company's name in the paper?"

"You know I do."

"It's too late for the Wheeler family to take part in the canvas auction. How do you feel about offering to fund the tarp?"

Gabe thought about the possibility as they approached the outbuildings. Melissa Faraday of Global News, with microphone in hand, was talking to the camera. He glanced at her, not wanting to garner her attention, but she saw him. *Crap!*

"Gabe, Gabe Bradshaw," she called, stalking toward him. "Why are you here today? Do you care to make a comment?"

He smiled, then strode toward her. "No comment, Miss Faraday."

"But why are you here? Is it true you intend to help the family?"

Gabe paused, hooked his fingers inside the belt loops of his denim jeans, and thought about her question. "One of my favorite artists, Lorne Hall, has a work of art in the silent auction. I'm thinking of placing a bid."

"Is that the only bid you're placing?"

"My dear Melissa," Gabe said with a grin, "what else would I bid on?"

"TarSan Oil is not known for human interest stories. There must be some reason—"

"Kit Wheeler," Gabe replied honestly, "and that's all you're getting from me. A good day to you, Miss Faraday."

"May I quote you?" she asked. Gabe nodded, winking, pressing forward.

"I don't know what your strategy is," Jared said, keeping stride with him, "but saying Kit's name, that was brilliant."

Gabe glanced at Jared. "I meant every word. I don't know the woman and she's already under my skin. Between you and me, I'm attracted to her story. I have no idea why."

A woman standing at the main roadway to the out-buildings passed each of them a brochure. She must have overheard their conversation as she appeared miffed. "Here's a map of the premises, sir. It will tell you where to go and how to get there."

She stared at him meaningfully.

Gabe disregarded her impertinence and her scowl. "When will the auction take place, the one where Miss Wheeler will be auctioned for a date?"

"Do you mean to make a bid?"

"I do."

"I know who you are."

"I gathered that. You have me at a disadvantage, Miss…"

"Mrs. Hemlock," she grunted, pursing her lips. "Mr. Bradshaw, the Wheelers are a good family. They've done a lot to help this community over the years."

"I'm sure they have."

"If you hurt that girl…"

"I'm not in the business of harming people, ma'am. If you'll point me in the direction of the main house?"

"It's on the map. If you're smart enough to punch a hole in the ground and drill for oil, you're smart enough to find the house."

Gabe couldn't help himself. He chuckled. "Thank you for your time, ma'am. Have a nice day."

"I love how you make an impression," Jared snickered, walking, scrutinizing the map.

"A real ladies' man," Gabe offered, shaking his head. "Let's not worry about it. As much as I'd like to change the world's opinion of the Bradshaw family, it's not likely to happen anytime soon."

"We'll give it a good try, Gabe. You convinced me."

"We've got a long way to go if we're to rethink the company directive and change opinions too. It's a new day. Let's get to this auction."

Gabe and Jared were soon seated in the first row, in front of the Wheeler house. "She sure told you," Jared laughed, digging out his cell phone.

"Irritating. Why does everyone despise the Bradshaw family? They couldn't drive their cars without us."

"It's the perceived environmental impact. Your dad doesn't want to embrace the possibilities of the future, but I'm telling you, to be successful, we have to consider the longtime costs of doing business. It's the only way. Breathe the air out here. Do you feel the difference with fewer vehicles? Gives a man something to think about."

"Lindsey keeps bringing up the same issues. Hope, too. But it's hard convincing the former president to entertain an entirely new plan."

"Let's not worry about it today. There's only one concern right now, and that's winning Kit Wheeler's bid."

"Whatever the cost?"

"You must win."

"LET THE SHENANIGANS BEGIN." Sam giggled, ready for the auction.

"Yeah, sure," Kit replied, standing in the doorway, not ready to face their patrons. Today was different. She was facing far more than the press. A multitude of guests waited, ready to purchase her family's belongings and their life story. Everyone desired a piece of the Wheeler family now and like her grandmother, she wasn't excited about seeing precious heirlooms disappear. She bit at her lip. What other choice did they have?

Sam had warned her of the type of gentlemen who could make a bid and she was worried about the after-effect. How had Sam talked her into this?

"Are you ready?" Samantha grinned, looking her straight in the eye.

"As ready as I'll ever be."

"Keep your eye on the prize, and the needs of the family in mind."

"I'm focused. I'm trying to do my part. I wish I had a million dollars, then I wouldn't have to go through with this auction."

"This moment could define your future. Our future."

"Maybe," Kit said, taking a deep breath. "I'm not convinced. Somehow, this story has become mine, the Kit Wheeler chick date rather than the plight of our family."

Samantha clutched her hand. "That's not true at all."

"Isn't it? It's my face plastered all over the place."

"Your image has made the difference and we're counting on you. We understand the stakes, and you're our project manager, so you have to take the lead. The picture with your sad expression, a plaintive girl standing by the pond, it captures the naked emotion we're feeling. The sadness. The loss. The distance we have to go to escape our debt. One image sells our story perfectly. It's hard for me to look at it without crying."

"I never imagined I'd have to stoop so low. I don't like fake business. I follow the line, the straight and the narrow."

Samantha released her hand. "There's nothing fake about you, or your image. Do you trust me, Kit?"

"It's not that I don't trust you."

"Look, cut the bullshit. Pull up your Wranglers and get outside. Greet the crowd from our front porch and appear as if you're ready to take on the world. We're taking Baby Blue to the track, and we need to earn the money to do it."

"It's a media circus."

"Yeah, it is," Sam exclaimed, sliding shaky fingers through her hair. "But, the way I see it, we've got this one shot. We've got to own it. Take the chance."

"Okay—"

Kit grasped the doorknob and pulled the door open. She glanced at her sister. "Do I have to wear the cowboy hat?"

"Oh, Kit." Sam giggled, her frown changing to a smirk. "It makes an impression."

"If I must," Kit growled, placing the beige hat on her head. She opened the door, hearing a shout rise from the crowd on the other side who were waiting for the auction to begin. She paused then, considering her sister. "I'll do it for you."

"Flash those pearly whites." Sam urged her through the front entryway and then closed the door.

KIT WHEELER SQUIRMED beneath the scrutiny of a hundred or more audience members, everyone watching her, some to place a bid and others perhaps more interested in watching the drama unfold. She felt awkward standing on her own front porch. The auctioneer, Chip Harkness, scrutinized her briefly, then peered at his prepared monologue and spoke into the microphone.

"Kit Wheeler comes from a proud family history of chuckwagon racing. Anyone can see her attributes. Beautiful baby-blue eyes just like her grandmother Dot's. Does anyone know? The baby-blue wagon was named after her grandmother's eyes. Isn't it appropriate a granddaughter would stand before you, having the courage to fight for the Wheeler cause? Give her a hand, folks."

"Whoop, whoop." Loud applause and a few whistles greeted her. Kit grinned as she was welcomed to her own front-porch stage. She didn't know why she glanced downward, shyly.

Chip encouraged the public to respond with more clapping. Kit listened to the applause, uncomfortable, squirming in her skin, taking in the attendees. One particular man sitting in the front row with nut-brown eyes and brown hair gained her attention. He winked.

"Now, I know you're ready to place your bids, but I want you to know what you're supporting. This family aims to ride again. To race Baby Blue on the Stampede circuit. You know what they'll need, right? A wagon can't race without the powerful muscles bred into thoroughbred horses, and a family can't buy horses without money. Never mind that there's a ranch to save, too. Are you ready to tender your bid, spend your well-earned dollars toward a worthy cause?"

Kit glanced at the auctioneer, then scrutinized Mr. Mysterious. He returned her ardor, staring directly at her. She'd seen such intensity before. A man who made known: *I'm gunning for you. I'm going to win.* Did she want him to?

"Now, she's not the prettiest filly…"

Kit swallowed her anger. How dare the auctioneer! She stepped toward the podium ready to take the mic from his smarmy hands and smack him in the head with it. He saw her coming; he laughed…

"…but I can see she's a spirited filly. Might need a real hero to break her in over a good dinner."

Kit was having none of it. She grasped his arm and whispered in his ear. "Get on with the bidding before I break you in."

She stepped back a pace, then smiled at the audience, waving. Her action received a few hoots and hollers, too. "Maybe Kit should drive Baby Blue instead of her brother, Cole. If she can manage the auctioneer, she can manage the horses."

The crowd applauded as if they agreed with the suggestion. Kit frowned, moving to her spot on the front porch.

"Hey, well, all right there, here we go," Chip announced, his voice taking on a sterner tone. "Who will give me one, bid one thousand dollars for this girl…"

Kit wasn't surprised when the man in the front row raised his hand. He didn't smile, he didn't frown, he sat on the bench with a focused expression appearing like he could afford the stakes. A heavy-set gent in the back row raised his hand, too, then another from the center.

"One-thousand-dollar bid. Now who will give me one-five. Do I have one-five?"

Mr. Mysterious raised his hand again. The bids kept climbing until the tally reached three thousand dollars.

Madness, Kit thought, squirming, watching nut-brown eyes raise his hand again and again. He was determined. He didn't even build a sweat. And then the bids stopped. Four thousand dollars?

"Come on, sir, you in the back row, don't let this gent in the front win a prize that should be yours? It's only money. And you, sir, you've got plenty. Will you give me four-five?"

He nodded.

"Who will give me five, five thousand dollars?"

The crowd quieted. The stakes were high. Mr. Mysterious raised his hand again. He didn't blink, nor did he raise an eyebrow. Who was this man?

"I'm out," the bidder in the last row called. "Save your rant, auctioneer."

"Going once? Going twice…"

"Sold—" Chip warbled, striking a gavel on the podium, his voice echoing. "To the man in the front row."

The man raised his hand, waving, smiling. Smiling? What did he want from her? Kit grasped the brim of her hat, and tipped her head at him, acknowledging her acceptance of the bid. Then she turned on her booted heel and escaped into the house.

Cole stood in the doorway at the ready. She'd never seen him dressed so spectacularly before. If she didn't know it, she'd think he was wearing new Wranglers. New Wranglers? Who gave him permission to buy new clothes? Jeans were not in the budget.

"Cole, is that you?"

"I know what you're thinking, Kit, that this is some kind of media show, but I haven't had a date in a long time. I want to make a good impression. How does a man meet a woman when all he does is work with cows?"

"They're ready for you, Cole," Samantha said. "Don't make him nervous, sis."

Kit's breath caught in her throat, when she witnessed the lack of confidence in her brother's eyes. His sadness nailed her right in the heart. Sad, because he was a good man. Any woman should want him.

"Who am I to keep a good man down." She placed her fist on his shoulder. "Go get her, bro, and good luck to you, too."

Cole grinned, then placed his hat on his head and stepped outside and onto the front porch. Kit sighed with relief. It was over, for now.

The door opened, and Kit turned toward the sound, wondering why Cole was returning.

"Cole?" But it wasn't Cole.

"Mr. Mysterious," Kit murmured, trying not to seem surprised. "Who are you?"

She should have been afraid with this man barging into her home, but she wasn't. She found herself struggling for words, not knowing what to say.

Jared had tried to stop him, but Gabe had grinned at his

47

employee like a journalist in pursuit of a hot story. He'd rushed toward the house, climbing four stone steps and crossing a wide covered verandah in record speed. It was the perfect moment to seek the woman's attention when the next bid was coming through the door. The brother stared at him, not knowing what to do.

"It's all right," he grinned, grasping Cole Wheeler's hand and shaking it firmly. "I've won a date with your sister. I want to introduce myself and make plans for the occasion."

Cole nodded and let him pass.

Soon standing inside the foyer of the house, Gabe could see that Kit Wheeler had already removed her Western hat. She was surprised to see him, too.

"Who invited you inside the house? I'm grateful for your bid, but coming inside uninvited, well, it's impertinent, don't you think?"

He grinned, getting right to the point. "I like a spirited filly. Look, Miss Wheeler. It is Miss, isn't it?"

"Mr. Mysterious, you bid on a date. Not insight into my personal life."

Gabe stood there, wondering best how to approach this woman. A hesitancy in her blue eyes, a raised scaredy-cat posture, but her shoulders rolled backward in defeat before he considered giving chase, causing him to inch forward in sympathy.

"This is the first time in my life I've made a bid on a date. I hardly know what to explore here, but I'm a businessman. When I see potential, I go after it. Look, I was drawn to your family's story and I wanted the date with you."

"Why?" she responded. "I'm curious to know your reasoning."

Kit Wheeler crossed her arms and stared at him like his mother used to when he was a boy. When he'd fought with his sister or acted badly. Yet only the tiniest amount of guilt consumed him, having forced his way inside her home. Risk was a part of life. He was comforted when she smiled.

"To be honest," Gabe replied, scrutinizing her baby-blue eyes, "we can help each other."

Mrs. Wheeler, the family matriarch walked into the adjoining room, interrupting their conversation.

"Is the auction over?" she said matter-of-factly, staring at each of them.

"Yes," Kit replied, sighing.

"Is this the man who won your bid?"

"Yes again, Gran."

"Well, don't keep him waiting at the front door. The Wheeler family might be down on their luck, but the way I see it, this man has offered you an olive branch. You could at least be grateful and invite him inside."

Gabe felt uncomfortable watching the confrontation. A look of annoyance crossed Kit's face and caught him in the gut. "It's all right, ma'am. I didn't mean to intrude."

"I'm sorry. I don't know what your name is." Kit tilted her head.

"Gabe," he said, reaching for her hand. "Gabe Bradshaw."

Kit accepted his grasp, holding his hand. A jolt of emotion warmed his palm. He glanced at his fingers when she let go.

"Now that we've formally met, Mr. Bradshaw, would you like some tea, a cup of coffee, or something stronger? What is your drinking pleasure?"

"I wouldn't mind a glass of water."

"He looks like the coffee type to me," Dot Wheeler exclaimed, wearing a stern expression. "Come with me, Mr. Bradshaw. I'll chaperone you while my granddaughter gets you a cup."

A determined woman. He followed her from the front hallway to a living area.

"Take a seat." She spoke as if she were a drill sergeant. "Anywhere you like."

Gabe picked a spot on a leather lounge chair. Dot Wheeler sat on an old rocking chair. She scrutinized him, staring him in the eye, making him uncomfortable.

"I don't like this business," she griped, glancing away. "Silent auction, win-a-date with a Wheeler, a bake sale, a whining singer, and most of my belongings for sale. I don't like strangers roaming across my land," she stated, her lips pursing together, "poking their noses where they don't belong. That door," she quipped, pointing, "hasn't stopped opening and closing all day. Church people, old friends of John's— Damn busy bodies; a woman needs her peace and quiet."

"And here I am, intruding on your good company and home. Maybe I should be leaving."

She waved the thought away. "Don't be silly. You're the only excitement I've had all day."

Gabe chuckled into his hand. "I don't want you to feel obliged to entertain me."

"Didn't you win the bid?"

"Well, yes."

She gazed at him as if she was interrogating him. He crawled beneath her scrutiny. "To my knowledge, my granddaughter hasn't had a date in years. Spends all her time at the office. I'm grateful to you. You should stay for the evening meal. Seems to me, you paid for the right."

"Now, Gran," Kit said, walking into the room holding a mug. "That doesn't seem right. We've only just met."

Gabe decided he liked this family matriarch. Despite the troubles she was facing, he admired her strength of will, her spirit. He ignored his date. "Is this an invitation?"

"Yes," Dot Wheeler replied, finally smiling.

"I wouldn't want to impose on Mr. Bradshaw," Kit responded, passing him a mug. "I know we need to talk through the details, such as what time you'll pick me up, where you'll take me, and when you'll bring me back…"

She suddenly stopped talking and stared at him. Gabe smiled. Frack. She was more beautiful in person than in the paper.

"Why are you smiling?"

"For the life of me, I don't know, but I want to know. Understand what drew me to a family's trouble in the first place."

"You said it yourself, you're a business man. You're probably trying to benefit from my family's downfall."

"Oh, I don't think so, Kit. Gabe looks innocent enough to me." Granny winked at him.

"Gabe? Gran, despite the fact he's given our family a healthy advance, he's a stranger to us."

Gran stopped rocking and leaned forward in her chair. "Kit Wheeler. You're being ill-mannered after this gentleman paid good money for you. Everyone's a stranger when they first meet. If the two of you don't mind, I'll take myself back to my room, so you can make your plans. Gabe Bradshaw, I better see you at dinner."

"I'd love to, ma'am, but my colleague is waiting for me and I'm expected somewhere else tonight."

"Very well, then. Another time."

Gabe was quiet until she left the room. He glanced at the coffee in the mug. Black? He sipped it anyway. "Your grandmother is a determined woman."

Kit Wheeler sat on the couch across from him. She leaned forward and held her head in her hands as if she were in pain. Then peeked through her fingers and observed him directly.

"Mr. Bradshaw, may I call you Gabe?"

"I'd appreciate it if you would. May I call you Kit?"

"Yes," she replied, but he could sense her reservations.

"You know, Kit, I want to be honest with you. This is not a simple situation. I've never placed a bid on a date before."

"We're in a similar situation then for neither have I stood in front of an audience of men, feeling like a cow, or a horse in an auctioneer's ring."

"I like your determination," Gabe remarked. "Your purpose, your resolve."

"My Gran was right. I apologize for my unseemly behavior. I do appreciate your generous gift. Why did you bid on me? I'm not a beautiful woman."

"You have your qualities."

"Oh?" Kit seemed to mull over his statement, leaning forward. "Tell me about my character traits. What do you see?"

"A strength of mind that mirrors your grandmother's."

"My Gran means business. She says what's on her mind and doesn't hold back."

"I like the way your sandy-blonde hair sweeps back from your forehead. Soft. Satiny, almost bold."

"I suppose you'll tell me next how much you like my baby-blue eyes?"

"I do. Perhaps they drew me to you from the start."

She leaned backward on the couch, shaking her head. He could see she didn't believe him.

"Mr. Bradshaw, enough of this tomfoolery. I know who you are. We can stop playing games. You're not interested in my blue eyes, nor do you care about my will-power. Tell me, Mr. President of TarSan Oil, what do you want from me and this family?"

So, she knew who he was. He took another sip of coffee then placed the mug on the side table. The time had come to offer a proposal. He rose from the lounge chair and joined her on the sofa. She didn't shrink away from his proximity next to her, but the power in her eyes diminished. She couldn't hide the uncomfortable ache that shaded the hollows beneath her baby-blue eyes with gray. He glimpsed the lack of sleep, the worry. He took her hand in his grasp. Squeezed. He had to be careful, that type of look had cost many a man their independence.

"I want to help you, but…"

"You need an endowment in return," she ruminated, glancing

at her hand. "An allowance or gift to recompense your five-thousand-dollar investment."

He released his grasp. God, why had he taken hold of her hand in the first place? He couldn't tell her that her sad story might benefit his father's company. That helping her family could win favor with a greater audience who attributed events like one oil spill to TarSan Oil?

"I'm not asking you to have sex with me if that's what you're getting at. I want to make a difference—"

"Why are you here, Mr. President? I don't understand how our circumstances could benefit your company. And don't sit here scrutinizing me like that. Sad puppy dog eyes. You would never have placed a bid unless you could gain from the win."

"You're an intelligent woman, Miss Wheeler."

"We're no longer on a first name basis? Is that right?"

"Look, Kit…"

"Tell me the truth. I can take it."

Could she? Somehow, he didn't think so. He would have to bend the truth.

"Okay, truth. I liked the idea of how your family's story might benefit the Bradshaw interests if I won the bid. Create some curiosity in the minds of media hounds and their readers wondering why I placed a bid in the first place, though if I'm to be honest, I was drawn to your family's plight, no different than the crowd of well-wishers scouring your land for bargains."

"Do you mean it? Don't lie to me, Gabe Bradshaw."

"Don't treat me like I'm a four-year-old boy. I get enough friction from my mother."

"Maybe we should make plans for our date. After all, I can 'drill' you further about your true purpose then."

"What do you do for a living, Kit? You speak as if you're an unyielding lawyer type."

"I used to be a project manager for one of your competitors."

He grinned. "Which one?"

"Mr. Mysterious, when you tell me your secrets, I'll tell you mine."

"What do you like to eat, do you have a preference?"

"I'm all about the meat and you want to make a good impression. I'd say a steak house."

"Oh, Kit, I'm really looking forward to this date. I've never met someone with as much spunk. I'll pick you up next Saturday, at three?"

"I thought we'd eat in Longview."

"Oh, no. I get to choose where we dine." He glanced at his watch.

"Have somewhere to go?"

"Actually, yes," Gabe said, rising from the couch. "My associate is waiting outside, and we need to get back to the city."

"I'll see you out."

Kit Wheeler escorted him to the back entrance as the auction was still taking place. She opened the door.

"Thanks for the coffee, Kit."

"You're welcome."

He walked outside onto the back porch, then turned back to her.

"Kit?" he said, staring at her.

"Yes?"

"You have the most amazing blue eyes I've ever seen. I wasn't lying. Your eyes drew me to you from the start."

"You're not too difficult to look at either," she confessed, blushing. "And whatever your motive, I appreciate your donation to my family. See you on Saturday. Do drive safely back to Calgary."

"Kit?" he asked, turning back.

"Mr. Bradshaw?"

"You paint a pretty picture in those jeans!"

She shook her head, clearly blushing while closing the door.

Gabe smiled, and went in search of Jared, feeling like the fool she thought him to be. He was looking forward to Saturday.

CHAPTER 6

The Wheeler family had assembled for the evening meal, exhausted from the day's events. Gran had made a pot roast and it was well after six o'clock when they finally gathered in the dining room to enjoy the evening meal. Kit soon understood why supper was late when Gran's longtime friend, Bennet Dalton, joined them at the old and weathered heritage table.

"Come hell or high water," Gran stated, slicing her meat, "Baby Blue won't race again. I've asked Bennet to join us for dinner, hoping he'll talk some sense into my young 'uns."

"Well, thanks for coming, Bennet, but after all of the media attention, we'd look like fools if we didn't follow through with the race." Michael stared at his mother meaningfully. "Especially after declaring we're taking the wagon back onto the track?"

"Our entire media campaign rests on Baby Blue riding again," Sam said gently. "I thought we were all on side."

"No one listens to me, anymore. Just because I'm seventy-seven doesn't mean I don't have a say in what goes on around here."

"Thanks for inviting me to dinner, Dot. Needless to say, it's always a pleasure to be in your company and see your family, too. Even under these circumstances."

"Bennet, you know why you're here. Help me plead my case."

"Thanks for putting me on the spot," he chortled, his laughter rumbling in his chest. "It's nice to see all of you again, but I was hoping we'd talk about the issues after dinner, maybe over dessert or a shot of whiskey."

"I'd like you to talk about the complicating factors."

"Kids," he coaxed, eyeing them, "your ambition is no secret, and your grandmother has asked me to slow you down. Chuck-wagon racing is a dangerous sport. Dot has been aware of the risks for a long time. I'm sure you understand, a heavy price was paid by this family."

"We understand the issues," Kit replied, staring first at Cole and then Samantha. They both nodded in support. "But Baby Blue has earned our recognition. If she wins the race, we could earn funds to secure the ranch."

"No," Gran exclaimed, scrutinizing her grandchildren. "I won't live to see another family member hurt, maimed, or God forbid, killed. I'll have my way in this situation if I have to axe the wagon."

Bennet raised his hand in appeal. "Kids, you sound like John, your grandfather. He'd always get this look of fierceness before a race, and his eyes would flash with excitement. I'm sorry, Dot, but despite the tragedy, there were good moments. Exciting moments. Hell…"

"Stop it. I didn't ask you here to talk about the good ole times, bringing your exploits to this table. Talking about a time when you were John's outrider."

"You're damn right," Bennet quipped, venting his anger. "And I liked my position on the team. Dot, I understand your concern but don't minimize our time together. True enough, I was John's outrider. His friend. I supported the man until the day he died." He grabbed his fork and stabbed a mouthful of roast. "You're a good woman. A good cook, too. If I hadn't already been married to Betsey Sue, I would have courted you myself after the accident."

"Now, Bennet…"

"Let me finish. I'm not a fool. I understand your concern, your worries, but I'll not be a trump card to make life happen the way you want it to."

"If you're not willing to help me, then why did you come here?"

"Good question. If truth be known, I'm here for John."

"Now you intrigue me," Michael Wheeler piped up, leaning forward. "What the hell is that supposed to mean?"

"I promised John I'd watch over this family and I've done my best while caring for my own."

"We're grateful to you," Michael responded, "especially your care in the early years. Hell, you've been a father to me."

"Look," Bennet said with a grimace, "John died living the life he loved. He understood the risks and the rewards. He would want the family assembled at this table to be mindful it was an accident that took his life."

Kit had been silent until now, but she could see that whatever Bennet was trying to say, his story was important, and she wanted to know more.

"What should we know?" Kit asked.

"This isn't a game. The half mile of Hell has a heritage of its own, and while you may want to hold the reins, racing Baby Blue to the finish line, well…, everyone assembled here must understand the cost involved."

"Like the loss of my husband," Gran growled, fierce as ever. Kit had never seen her grandmother like this before.

"We won't get hurt, Gran."

"Cole, you cannot make such a promise to your grandmother," Bennet pointed out, glowering at Kit's brother. "You're the appointed driver, right? You must consider the would-be hurt to yourself, injury to your horses, maybe your outriders, too. There could be human costs to bear, animal ones, too. If a horse stumbles and falls, breaking a leg, breaking its neck, can you hold a gun to its head and pull the trigger? Can you?"

Everyone looked at each other, the uncertainty evident on their faces. No one had an answer for Bennet's rant, so Kit posed the question.

"Bennet, have you ever seen a horse put down?"

"Yes. But not while on the track."

"What was my grandfather's position on racing?"

"God love him, John understood the risks. He loved his cart, his horses, his wife, and the child he knew was coming, but he never saw himself beneath the wagon's wheels. That's a painful image I've had to live with my entire life. Like your grandmother, I don't want history to repeat itself." He studied each of them. "I need to protect John's offspring."

"Bennet, we appreciate you coming here to talk to us, but we need to make this decision as a family. What are we to do? Should we take Baby Blue back to the track or is this an ill-informed idea we should let go?"

"It would be a media disaster," Sam stated, shaking her head. "We've had people cross our land. We don't have to win, but we do have to race the wagon. I'm sorry if this news bursts anyone's bubble, but I'm not backing down."

"Me neither," Cole agreed.

"No." Gran was as determined as ever.

Sam and Kit didn't see eye to eye often, but in this instance, her beautiful sister with strawberry-blonde hair was right. They had to push forward, but educated on the risks so they would be safe.

"Accidents happen but I'm still in, for the sake of the ranch." Kit scrutinized Samantha, then Cole. "If any one of us feels we shouldn't do this, I'll stand down from my position."

"I'm in," Cole replied. "I can drive the wagon; I've driven one plenty of times. And for the sake of Gran's worries, I'll study safety options."

"Me, too," Sam agreed.

Bennet smiled, slapped his hand on the table. "Well, I'll be damned. Now this is exciting."

"I didn't think you wanted the family to race again," Michael Wheeler said with a laugh. "Why are you smiling?"

"Because John would be whooping, hollering, and carrying on right now, seeing his family not willing to go down the shit hole without a fight."

"Will you help us, Mr. Dalton?" Kit asked. "I suspect you learned a trick or two racing with our grandfather. If we're to do this, we want to do it the right way, with the right lessons. We'll need a mentor."

"You bet, I will."

"Bennet!" Gran quipped, rising from the table. "I didn't bring you here so you could get involved with this craziness. Mentor my grandkids? I won't let you."

"Dot, honey, if I can't talk your family out of their dreams of winning, then I'm damn well going to help them succeed, and ensure no one gets hurt."

"What are you saying?" Kit asked.

"I'll mentor you. I know how far you have to go to win the half mile. I know what you'll need."

"Money," Michael remarked. "Does anyone know how much we earned today?"

Sam grinned. "Twelve thousand from the date auction alone. The funds might buy us a few thoroughbreds."

"How many horses will we need?" Cole asked.

"Twenty, give or take a few."

"Why so many?" Kit asked, surprised at the amount.

"Well—" Bennet scratched his head. "You need horses that are comfortable in different track conditions. Some specially trained to run when the track is wet, some when it's dry."

"We can't afford that many. We have two mortgage payments to make."

"You might be able to get by with twelve."

"And how are we to transport twelve horses? We only have one trailer."

"I can help you with an extra trailer, but you'll need at least three, and people to drive them, too."

"We've got a long road ahead of us," Kit offered, feeling deflated all of a sudden.

Michael Wheeler calmly placed his cutlery by the side of his plate. "Seems to me we need someone to sponsor us. Kit, maybe you could convince Gabe Bradshaw to be our benefactor."

"Dad, I'm obligated to a date and nothing more."

"You'll need a tarp for the wagon, Kit. Mr. Bradshaw's a businessman. You're beautiful, but he wants more than a date with you."

"Dad…"

"Tell you what…" Bennet laughed, staring at Michael and Kit. "The three of us should have a discussion tomorrow. Go over the financial needs of the ranch and the race, then you'll have facts to propose to Mr. Bradshaw."

"But why would he want to help us? He's already paid five thousand dollars."

"Because he's looking for an investment and the family is in the news."

"Okay, so if he says yes. What do we have to offer him in return?"

"The company name, TarSan Oil, on the tarp."

"Aha," Sam retorted, "and then we'd invite the Bradshaw family, maybe a few of their employees as well, to come into the inner circle of the Wheeler family. Visit the ranch, maybe? More photo opportunities for social media to keep us in the news."

"This is getting exciting," Cole marveled, smiling.

In the family's excitement, no one noticed the sadness that had come over Dot Wheeler's face. Kit perused her grandmother, her head dipped and silent tears leaking from her eyes. A horrible look of defeat crumpled her face. She raised her head and calmly pushed her chair back from the table.

"I pray," she choked, swallowing her pain, "that history does not repeat itself."

She escaped from the room.

"Don't worry about your grandmother," Bennet said, he too rising from the table. "I'll take care of her."

When the five of them were alone, Kit asked the question. "Are they a couple?"

Her father smiled. "I suspect they always have been, but with Betsey passing away last spring, well, I'm surprised Bennet hasn't popped the question. They're together almost every day…"

"And night," Gina hastened to add, finally finding her voice. "Everyone deserves their own slice of heaven. I've sat here listening to you and no different than Gran, I'm a mother. I don't want my family members hurt, but I'll support you, if this is what you want. Is it? Because we could still sell the ranch."

"We're not having this discussion again," Michael said to his wife.

Mom stared at them, gauging their expressions. She accepted the outcome in her own way, smiling slimly, nodding her head.

"How about some coffee?" she asked, rising from the table. "I made a peach cobbler, too. Would anyone like some?"

"Yes, please. You know how to make us happy, Mom."

"Every mother only wants the best for her family and I know you understand this, too."

Mom relished having the final word. Gave her family a mindfulness to take into their future.

CHAPTER 7

*G*abe thought about his business options as he drove. What should he discuss with Kit Wheeler first? He hoped to propose TarSan Oil sponsor the family's chuckwagon ambitions and he considered such options as a canvas for the wagon, maybe horses and who knew what else, too. He wondered how she'd feel about aligning her family initiatives with his ideas? He'd have to travel a few more miles to find out.

He focused on the road ahead while reflecting on the woman he would soon pick up, and he smiled in contemplation. He was excited to see Kit Wheeler.

He exited the highway traveling west along a side road, and soon drove the fenced pastures of Wheeler land. He glanced at cattle grazing, taking in the scenery. He smiled, seeing the odd calf frolicking, kicking up its hooves. Without the hundreds of cars from days before, the sight was amazing. He drove along their driveway, parked his car, and then walked to their front entrance.

This time, he knocked instead of barging inside. Kit opened the door. "Hi, Mr. Bradshaw."

"Wow!" Gabe grinned, taking in her appearance. "I hardly recognize you, wearing a peach ruffle dress. You've gone classic.

What happened to the Western girl, the woman wearing a Western shirt, jeans and a cowboy hat?"

"You remember all that?" she asked, leaning against the doorjamb, smiling.

"A man could hardly forget how we first met."

Sandy blonde hair swept back from her forehead and was tied at the nape of her neck. He studied rose-gold earrings dangling beneath her earlobes and a fresh face powdered with light makeup. She was pretty.

"Mr. Mysterious, you're taking me out for dinner. A woman dresses for the occasion, but, what exactly are you wearing?"

"You don't like my clothing? I dressed comfortably, in jeans, a T-shirt and a blazer, thinking you'd dress country."

"I see," she mused, staring at his eyes, glancing at his chest and then perusing his jeans like a mare considering a stallion. He shook his head, not expecting such a reaction.

"Underdressed?" he asked, attracted to her serene expression, her strong cheek bones. Nothing austere to be found. He practically forgot why he'd come.

"Maybe I should change?" She gestured toward her clothing. A pearl bangle dangled at her wrist. "Doesn't matter to me where you take me for dinner. Would you like to come inside? Have a shot of whiskey before we go? It's all the craze in the hills?"

"Blue eyes, we should hit the road. It's an hour drive back to Calgary and I want to treat you right."

"Well then, come inside and I'll get my purse, and then we can be on our way."

Gabe stepped inside the entranceway and watched Kit as she retrieved a camel-colored sweater. She reached for a pair of matching high heels, then sat on a nearby chair to put them on. He swallowed, taking in long, well-shaped legs.

"I could help you," he offered.

Her eyebrows rose. "Like a prince would assist his Cinderella? It's hardly a glass slipper."

He didn't ask for her permission. He knelt before her wondering perusal and grasped her shoe, assessing her expression, then slipping the stiletto on her foot, his fingers lingering against her ankles.

"It's okay to breathe," he said, his fingers sliding along her silk stockings. He reached for the other shoe and slipped it on the other foot.

"I don't think anyone has helped me with my shoes since my mother tried to assist me with my laces in early childhood, much to my teacher's chagrin. By chance, are you good with foot massages, too?"

Gabe smiled, glancing upward, enjoying the sparkle in her eyes. In this peach dress with a touch of blush staining her cheeks, he likened her to a stunning flower. He rose from the plank floor and reached for her hand, urging her to rise. "Are you requesting a foot massage?"

She blushed, her face crimson. "It's too soon for such intimacy, right?"

"I invested in a date, but I'm open to exploring our options."

"Let's see where our conversation takes us." She grasped his arm, meeting his eyes. "I'm thirty, after all. Not a girl anymore. Suddenly," she said, appraising him again, "I'm looking forward to our evening together. Where will you take me?"

He opened the door and escorted her outside, feeling her fingers where she clutched his arm. "Where would the lady like to go? What do you like to eat?"

"I'm partial to seafood."

"You are? A girl like you raised on a cattle ranch, I would have thought good ole Alberta beef would be your food of choice."

Her heels clicked against the wood planks as they passed across the porch. "I don't mind a good steak from time to time." He escorted her across a crushed-gravel walkway and led her to his car. "I prefer mine cooked medium. Well done destroys the texture."

He opened the passenger door. "Kit, you and I will get along just fine."

She climbed inside his vehicle and into his life, already under his skin. "Mr. Bradshaw, you're a gentleman. Suddenly, I'm looking forward to this date."

"Me, too."

Gabe smiled, wondering what was happening between them.

WHEN THEY REACHED OKOTOKS, Kit couldn't take the suspense any longer. She'd been quiet most of the ride and was uncomfortable sitting inside his BMW. A sexy silver car with a white leather interior, it breathed luxury and wealth, everything she couldn't have. She appreciated the raw smell, but she didn't belong inside a car like this. She gazed at the man at the wheel, who seemed comfortable in her presence, realizing she wanted to belong somewhere and to someone. He glanced at her and smiled.

"I see the wheels turning in your head. What are you thinking about?"

"Honestly?"

"I expect nothing less."

Kit stretched, then glanced outside the window, considering the passing fields. "I like this car. I could become accustomed to the comfort. What did it cost, if you don't mind me asking?"

"Forty thousand or so, give or take a few. It's a comfortable all-season vehicle. You in the market for a new ride?"

"Would I be sitting in your car, having been auctioned off for a date, if I could afford such a prize?"

"By the sound of your voice, I suspect not. I'm sorry. I should have known better than to ask the question."

"Look, Gabe," Kit said, sighing. "The Herald's article was pretty clear on my family's state of affairs. Why did you bid on me? For that matter, why did you come to the auction?"

He glanced at her momentarily and then returned his attention to the highway. She watched long lean fingers massage the leather-wrapped steering wheel. "Honestly, I couldn't throw the newspaper away."

"What?"

"The newspaper. The one with your image."

"How fascinating. Tell me more. I don't think any man has ever responded to my likeness in the way you describe."

"You know, I'm not a man who's easily overcome by journalistic accounts, but I held the Herald in my hand and studied your portrait, and…"

"And what? It's a terrible image of me. I look like a boy."

"Oh, honey." He glanced at her, his eyebrows rising. "You shouldn't have such a low opinion of yourself. I sure as hell didn't see a boy standing in the pasture. I saw…"

"Tell me what you saw, now you have me wondering if I've been wrong about myself all these years."

"Well, a woman, with sadness and struggle dimming the light in her eyes. The sunset in the background, falling beneath the horizon, and you peering at the camera's lens as if you were falling with it. If you'd smiled, you'd have lit the scenery with emotion. But the stoic expression, the sadness, tore at my heartstrings."

His words took Kit back to the moment when the portrait was taken.

"Don't smile at the camera, Kit. Look into the setting sun if you have to, that falling ball of light represents our family, and the foreclosure we'll suffer if we don't get this right."

Kit didn't want to think about foreclosure or sadness. She wanted to enjoy this date.

"What are you thinking about? I see I've upset you. I didn't mean to make you sad."

"It's not you. I was remembering my sister, Sam. In charge of" the camera, she was good at getting me to pose. She kept nagging, snapping shot after shot until… Damn it, it felt so fake." Kit sighed, staring. "You know, all I wanted from the media attention was a way to save my family's ranch. I have to know, are you interested in helping us?"

"I made a healthy bid at the auction. Money changes everything."

"Yes," Kit replied, realizing he sounded sincere, "but a man like you, driving a car like this, five thousand dollars is a drop in the bucket."

"Look, I might be the president of TarSan Oil, but let me assure you, the company's funds are not limitless. They're managed carefully. My father," Gabe sighed, expelling a breath, "takes no pleasure in waste, and manages everything to do with his business carefully."

"You're frowning."

"It's nothing."

"Now you've made me curious."

"My father wasn't supportive of this venture."

"He must have agreed to it, but why would he approve of an auction if what you say is true?"

"It's simple," Gabe said, shaking his head, "I have not been on a real date in months. My father was affronted when I recently went to a movie by myself, so…"

"By yourself? I have to agree with your father. That's sad. But let me get this straight. Your father was not impacted by a family in trouble, he only wanted you to have a date? Is that right?"

"I didn't say he didn't care."

"You didn't have to." Kit gazed outside again. She knew most people had a motive for everything they did in life. What was Gabe's? He kept his truth well-hidden.

"Do you think I'm lying?"

"No. That kind of story," Kit said, glancing back, "can't be made up."

"I have to admit, I didn't like visiting the theater by myself or watching the movie alone."

"You're a handsome guy. Do I dare ask why there isn't a girl on your arm?"

"You're wrong on that accord. Tonight, there is a woman capturing my attention and I assure you, she's not a girl."

Kit smiled. "Who is this woman?"

"I plan to find out."

THEY FINALLY REACHED Calgary's city limits. Kit was quiet as Gabe drove northbound on Macleod Trail, east on Canyon Meadows Drive, and then south on Bow Bottom Trail. Soon, they drove a single track of roadway where poplar trees lined either side. Kit knew they had entered Fish Creek Park.

"Where are you taking me, Gabe?"

"Have you never been to Fish Creek Park?"

"I'm not dressed appropriately for a nature hike or a picnic, so I hope walking through the forest is not your idea of a date."

"Well, honey, we could take a walk after dinner, if you want, but I have other plans. We're dining at Bow Valley Ranche House. It's quaint, quiet and private; a place where we can have good conversation and get to know each other better while enjoying a glass of wine and a good meal. Have you been before?"

"Once or twice."

"Good. Then you know what you're in for."

He parked the car. Kit waited as he stepped outside. He soon opened the passenger door, offered his hand, and helped her exit the vehicle. "Thank you. I could get used to this. Not every man opens a door for a lady."

"My father taught me my manners."

"Maybe I'll meet him sometime. If there's a second date?"

She grasped his arm beneath the elbow. "I could be persuaded to introduce you if the evening goes well."

"I'll be on my best behavior." Kit laughed, squeezing his arm. "You've chosen well for a destination."

"Suits my purpose for what I have to propose."

"Oh, yeah, and what is that?"

"There's plenty of time. Let's wait until we've each enjoyed at least one glass of wine."

"Sounds serious. I hope I won't be disappointed."

Kit knew what the warning meant but she didn't care right now. She was enjoying Gabe Bradshaw's easy manner and didn't want the evening to end. In his company, her troubles seemed far away and that's the way she liked life right now.

After they were seated near the fireplace and the server brought her favorite wine, a German Riesling, Kit sipped the vintage, enjoying the subtle taste of apple, and all too often, staring at Gabe. He broke off a piece of bread. She watched him place a bite-sized piece in his mouth. Watched his lips moving as he chewed. He was a handsome man.

"I'm not sure I want to know what you're thinking?"

Kit giggled. "I'm not sure I want to tell you."

"Kit Wheeler, if I didn't know better…"

"Gabe Bradshaw, I'm about to embarrass myself, but I'm offering my appreciation anyway… You're a damn fine specimen of a man."

He smirked, choked on his bread, and would have made a genius reply but the server arrived with their salads. Poached pear and baby kale for her, beet root and smoked salmon for the gentleman. Kit didn't rush to eat her salad. She reached for her goblet and took another sip, contemplating, savoring, smiling.

Gabe stretched forward. "You like what you see?"

"I do."

She glanced at his right hand, studied his index finger sliding along his fork. "I'm not sure I should tell you what thoughts are pressing my attention."

"If I'm playing the fool, or if you don't feel the same attraction, please just lie to me. I'm enjoying your company and couldn't bear for this date to be spoiled. I know you paid for our time together, but…"

She placed her wine glass on the table. He stretched forward and took hold of her fingers. His touch was warm, the tenderness exhibited from his amber eyes, steadfast and true. He didn't look away. An electrical current shot up her arm.

"You're beautiful, Kit. So pretty in your peach dress. Your face is alight with joy. No sadness to be found. Now we're only getting to know each other, so your cheeks suffusing with pink could be a natural reaction from the wine. And I'm not relating your attributes merely because I'm thinking about what it might feel like to sleep with you. I honestly want to know more about the Western girl I bid on."

Kit swallowed, pulled away from his touch, her face suddenly warm. "A bold statement."

"Look, I don't think you'll disagree, we're making a connection."

"I won't deny it," Kit breathed, contemplating. "I like being here with you, but any girl would. You're the complete package. Mr. Mysterious driving a luxurious car, the benefactor of an amazing meal, offering me my favorite wine…"

"I like it when you call me your little pet name. Makes me feel like James Bond in the flesh. No one has done that before."

"No one?"

"It's good for my ego." Gabe lifted his fork, then stabbed a wedge of salmon and placed it in his mouth. "It tastes good, too, going down, if you know what I mean."

Kit followed suit, enjoying the flavor combination of pear, pecan, and pomegranate vinaigrette as much as she enjoyed his suggestive words. She shied away from his perusal; his lips as he sipped red wine seemed even more heated. Full. Firm. This was happening too fast. She had to change the topic.

"I know you have a greater purpose than this meal. Perhaps we should talk about your real intentions?"

"Whatever they are, they're forgotten."

"Oh, I don't think so," Kit said with a slight smile. "Whatever brought you to the auction lurks beneath the surface, waiting to steal into our conversation."

"I'm not a thief. I want to help you."

"How do you propose to further finance your bid?"

He appeared so calm as he ate, carefully partaking of his salad, glancing at her while he chewed. He didn't rush the conversation as if there was no need. "Are you sure you want to talk business?"

"It's a business discussion, then?"

"Don't look so crushed. Business is what led me to you, and that…"

"Picture…" Kit finished for him, having known all along that a man didn't spend five thousand on a dinner date without wanting a gift in return. "Lay it on me, Mr. Bradshaw."

"Kit, I want to be honest with you. You seem like a woman who wouldn't accept less."

"I appreciate an honest man. I don't revel in people who lie to me. So please don't."

"I was drawn to your story, your picture. I've told you as much but helping your family could prove beneficial for the company's brand."

"Tell me more."

"Since the oil spill…"

"I'm aware of the challenges your company has faced."

"Kit, I've only been president for a few months and I want to make changes."

"Changes to your company's bottom line or its image?"

"Our image for starters and helping your family might bring

good attention to our brand. Maybe trolls might say something positive for a change."

"Probably won't make a difference, actually. People can be mean. And unkind. Even in the direst of circumstances. My sister, Sam, opened a Facebook page. She's had to ban some negative fans from it."

"That's terrible. I cannot even bring myself to spend much time on social media any longer for fear of what I might read. What some inconsiderate uneducated person might say. I have not had a date in a long time as…"

"You can tell me."

"Well, Kit, who would date a man whose company is responsible for damaging the environment?"

Kit scrutinized the worry lines creasing his forehead. The concern reflected in his nut-brown eyes. He placed his fork on his plate and stretched backward. The loll in his posture connected with her own sorrow and she desired to lift his spirits up.

"I'd like to date you."

He glanced at her, clearly thinking. "Have we met before, Kit Wheeler?"

"Not to my knowledge."

"Crazy, 'cause I feel like we've had this conversation before. Like I know you. I want to talk business, mostly, but I'm distracted."

"Focus." She licked her lips. "Tell me what you were going to say."

"I want to help your family; however, I need a return on my investment."

"Okay. Don't tell me what you want to do, show me. I need to hear more than platitudes if I'm to consider a partnership," Kit stressed, nodding her head.

"Is your family serious about racing the chuckwagon?"

Kit nibbled at her lip, glanced away. "It was Sam's idea. Cole is crazy excited about the prospect and we made a good profit from the sale, but a lot of money will need to go to the debt, to hold off our creditors."

"But your family, you're seriously taking the wagon back to the track."

"Yes. I feel like I can trust you, or I wouldn't share this," Kit disclosed, staring at Gabe. "At first, the idea was more of a lark. I don't think anyone was serious about racing, but now, the Wheelers are fired up. Well, everyone but my grandmother."

"You'll need funds to purchase items, like a tarp for the wagon."

"Aha," Kit declared, reaching for her goblet, "you want to invest in the canvas, maybe put TarSan Oil's name on it?"

"Yes. If you're okay associating with a man whose company is responsible for an oil spill."

"Did you clean it up?"

"We've tried to. We're undertaking an impact study to see how we can positively affect the environment and studying our operations to ensure a spill won't happen again, but researching solutions takes time."

"I'll have to talk to my family. See how they feel about your offer."

"Are you finished with your plates?" the server interjected.

"Yes," they each replied.

"Your main course will be out soon."

"I'm looking forward to it." Kit sighed, but didn't say more until the server was gone.

"I'm sure you know my family has no choice but to accept your offer and for what it's worth, I believe your intentions are well-meaning."

"You do? Why are you smiling, Kit?"

"This won't be our only date. I'll get to see you again."

"I have not asked you yet."

"No. But you will."

Gabe Bradshaw reached for his wine-glass, a red Merlot, opposite of her white. He held the goblet to her and she clinked his glass. "Cheers."

"To the next occasion…"

"To our future partnership. To success. To Baby Blue winning the half mile of Hell."

"For the win!" Kit agreed, sipping her wine.

She licked her lips, suddenly seeing an upside to the family struggles. She didn't want this evening to end any time soon. Modesty was the only reserve that stopped her from leaving her seat at the table and wrapping Gabe Bradshaw in a firm and grateful hug.

CHAPTER 8

*K*it was quiet for most of the drive back to the ranch. She glanced at Gabe from time to time, studying his brown hair, his five-o-clock shadow, and she'd smile when he'd glance at her, seeming to share her curiosity. She did not want this evening to end. Every part of their time together had been enjoyable.

A storm was brewing on the horizon. Dark clouds were rolling in. They'd barely seen the sun set. Suddenly, a zigzag current of light flashed across the twilight sky, quickly followed by the rumble of thunder. It seemed like the sky was about to release its burden.

"Looks like we've made it back before the rain." Kit glanced at Gabe as he drove along the family driveway.

"I enjoyed our evening together. Don't really want a beautiful night to end."

"I know it's late, but would you like to come inside?"

He put the car in park and turned off the ignition. "I can't stay, but I'll walk you to the door." And like before, he exited the vehicle and came around to her side.

Boom! The sound of thunder crackled and rumbled, the discordant sound jarring the elements, causing Kit to shiver. Gabe

75

opened the door and reached for her hand. She accepted his grasp, smelling the precipitation in the air; the first droplets spitting against her face.

"We better hurry, it's falling…"

Hand in hand, they raced across the crushed gravel together, laughing. Kit felt young, the moisture against her skin was welcome, the strength holding her hand better still and necessary. She was soon climbing the porch steps to pause on the landing, facing Mr. Mysterious.

Gabe held her hands. "I want to see you again, talk about our plans."

The thunder boomed. Out of the corner of Kit's eye, she saw another streak of lightning and maybe the curtain in the window drawing aside. "Come inside? I'll make you a cup of coffee."

"It's late."

Suddenly, the rain began to fall. Kit didn't like thunderstorms. Frightened, she froze on the verandah, wanting to go inside, but not wanting to leave this man just yet. A moment in her life when she'd found herself wishing for a love she'd never known. She didn't have the will to say goodbye.

"It's raining. You'll get wet if you walk into it."

He squeezed her fingers. "Kit, it's only water and we've only just met."

"I know, but, I don't have the 'will' to say goodbye."

She gazed upward, scrutinizing warm brown eyes. There was this silent awkward pause, but then he sighed and pulled her near his chest. She went willingly into his arms, welcoming his embrace.

"Seems like the gods don't want me to leave, either."

Kit closed her eyes, leaning closer, breathing the musky scent of a man and his leather jacket. She gripped the rawhide in her fist. She hadn't been with a man in a long time and she didn't care which family member might be watching.

"I don't want you to leave."

Beep. Beep. Kit heard the car doors lock.

Gabe took a step back, but he held her still in a partial hug. "Too much rain to take a chance. I'll accept the coffee after all, until the storm passes. Look, Kit, I feel like there's a connection between us."

"Yes, I feel it, too, and I like it!"

Kit stepped away but grabbed Gabe's hand. She opened the door and ushered him inside the Wheeler home. "If the rain doesn't let up, you can stay the night, if you want to."

He paused at the threshold. She witnessed the bewilderment in his eyes. "This is moving too fast."

"Perhaps," Kit said, "but we have not won the race yet. Come. Let's start with the drink I promised. See where the heat takes us."

"Honey, I'm thirsty for a sweetness other than liquid."

"The family is probably still awake," she grinned, squeezing his hand, wondering where the interloper had retreated to. "If we went to the office, no one would know."

He went quiet. Kit searched his expression, wondering what risks he was prepared to take. She herself was entertaining a dangerous pursuit. Should they? Would they?

"The hell with it," Kit moaned, grabbing his hand. "Let's go."

"Go?" he laughed, as she ushered him back into the night. "Where? We're going to get wet?"

"Who cares," Kit replied, removing her heels, then escorting him down the stairs and into the rain. "You might not need your clothes anyway."

He broke into a fit of laughter as they raced across wet grass and then a muddy road, together, soon finding themselves standing inside the office space of a building, separate from the main house, alone. When the door closed, Gabe held her again, taking her into his arms. Kit reached to him, sliding her fingers along his wet cheek, then pulling him nearer to her lips.

"I've been waiting to taste you all night," Gabe muttered, a throaty growl in his throat.

"Kiss me then," she said.

The thunder struck again but she was safe inside. She dropped her shoes on the floor. Gabe wiggled his feet out of his. His hands on her back. Her hands in his chocolate hair.

"I have not had a man in a long time, I hardly know what to..."

"Stop talking," he breathed, as she led him up the stairs to the bedroom, "I'm about to rock your world."

She paused midstride in the middle of the staircase to pull him close and kiss his mouth. She couldn't seem to break away from his heat. Leaving his warmth, she licked her lips, slid her hand along his back, squeezing the rounded curve of his buttocks.

"Oh darling. Where do we go from here?"

He picked her up. Kit wrapped her arm around his broad shoulders and leaned into his neck, kissing his skin. "Down the hallway to the end. There's a bedroom there."

Finding his way in the darkness, he carried her to the bed and laid her on the counterpane. Kit reached for him and pulled him close, kissing his lips again. He stood above her, staring, studying her fervent expression.

"Are you sure you want this? I mean, is it too soon?"

Kit sighed, licked her lips. "You said you were taken by my portrait. That you liked my peach dress."

"True enough."

She pulled him back to her and kissed his lips. He leaned his forehead against hers. His fingers did little swirls against her peach fabric, bringing her nubs to life. "Take what you need, darling, you paid for it."

He went still. Very still. Kit was sorry the minute she uttered the statement, realizing what she had implied. She'd ruined the moment.

He left her embrace to sit on the edge of the bed.

"I'm sorry. I didn't mean it the way it sounded. Come back to me. Please don't leave."

He looked at her. "Kit?"

"It was sex-play, nothing more."

"I'm not the type of guy who sleeps with the first girl he meets." He placed his hand on her leg. "I don't want to give you the wrong impression."

"I'm not a loose woman either." Kit sighed, drawing her fingers through her hair. "But neither am I a virgin. Please, don't leave. Maybe our relationship is moving at the speed of light, but I have not been with anyone in a long time. You've opened the floodgates. I want to experience the fireworks. I want…"

He came back to her. He grasped her chin, holding her face in his hands. "I don't want to get burned. Fireworks can be explosive. I should leave."

"No. Please don't. Stay the night."

"I'll regret this in the morning," he foretold, rising from the bed. Kit watched him strip off his clothing, his blazer, white T-shirt and jeans, until he stood before her in nothing more than Spiderman boxers.

"Spiderman?" She giggled, rising from the bed.

"A gift from my mother." He joked, shaking his head, smiling. "I didn't expect to find myself in a compromising position."

He grabbed her hand and sashayed her in a pirouette, turning her as if they were dancing, then drew his fingers across her neckline, causing tiny shivers, her skin heightened by the possibilities. Without asking, he unzipped her dress, permitting the silky fabric to slide to the floor.

"Come to bed, darling." He squeezed her buttocks.

Kit swallowed, pausing to stare at his heated gaze, pondering the bulge in his shorts. Silent, she permitted this gentle bear to escort her back to bed. He lifted the covers, helped her to lie inside, then covered her.

"We're not having sex tonight."

"We aren't?"

"No. It's too soon."

She grasped his thigh, her fingers sliding the length of his skin to the bejeweled juncture between. She cupped him. She heard his groan. "You sure, Mr. Mysterious?"

"Aw, darling, do you always get your way?" he moaned, taking her mouth in a ravaging kiss, then climbing beneath the sheets. "A man can't say no to a woman in need and we only live once, right?"

"Right," Kit sighed, pulling him closer, grasping his lip with her teeth. "Make love to me, Gabe Bradshaw…"

"I aim to please, ma'am."

CHAPTER 9

When Kit awoke the next morning, she was alone in the bed. She glanced at the empty hollow in the sheets, glimpsing the indentation Gabe had left behind, feeling cold without him near, realizing her lover of the night before had silently left her side without so much as a thank you or a kiss goodbye.

She stretched backward in the bed, smiling. She'd never been loved by a man in the way Gabe Bradshaw had pleasured her. He'd taken joy in touching every inch of her body. The small of her back, the inner curve of her thigh, and the pleasurable places in between. She remembered the haunting look in his eyes, and his fingers…

Do you like this? This? Should I touch you here, or there?

Oh, sweet heaven, she was sure he'd left his mark on every inch of her body.

She left the bed and retrieved her peach dress from the floor. She would face an interesting commentary when she strolled into the house wearing clothing from the night before. She sighed, preparing for the questions, but in truth, she didn't care what her family thought. She was an adult, thirty years old for heaven's sake.

She dressed quickly, styling her hair as best she could without a brush, then remade the bed while pondering what might evolve from her evening escapade. If anything. Gazing back at the bedcovers longingly, she left the bedroom and retrieved her high-heeled shoes from the front entrance, then left the office to stand outside, to listen to the sparrows singing. The fresh scent of dew lay heavy on the grass and glistened on pink tea roses. Beautiful and fresh after a night of rain.

Approaching the house, she was surprised to see the BMW parked in the driveway. So, Gabe had not left yet.

"Have a good night?"

Sam sat in the shadows, swaying on the porch swing. "Yes, actually," Kit replied, grinning, "and I have you to thank for my pleasure."

"You're blushing, big sister. What trouble did you get up to last night?"

Kit disregarded the question. "Is Gabe inside the house, then?"

"Yes. Mr. Tall and Handsome was trying to escape, sight unseen, but Bennet caught him and invited him inside for breakfast."

"Bennet's here?"

"It's full steam ahead with the Baby Blue show, and Bennet is game to get some horses purchased."

"Nice talking to you, too, Sam, but I should get inside. Ensure Mr. Bradshaw doesn't get eaten alive."

KIT PLACED her heels in the closet. Hearing voices, she passed through the entranceway and into the dining room. Her father raised a coffee mug to his lips, giving her a look that promised a serious discussion. Dad wasn't one to hold back.

"Good morning, Kit," her mother quipped, giving her the eye. "Imagine how surprised your family was to see Mr. Bradshaw here this morning."

Gabe wisely didn't reply. Holding a fork in his hand, he shifted eggs around his plate, but he couldn't hide the discomfort wrinkling his expression. Kit grabbed an empty chair, eyed her lover of the night before, and then sat beside him. "Did you hear the thunder last night?" she mused, hoping to make light of the fact that Gabe was sitting beside her. "It was raining so hard we didn't think driving was safe. It was late. I couldn't let our benefactor leave with the weather the way it was. It wouldn't have been right."

"Is that so," her father asserted. "Where did the two of you sleep? I noticed your bed was empty this morning."

"Ahem," Gabe coughed into his hand, appearing uncomfortable.

"You know, Dad, I'm past the age of majority. Frankly, it's none of your business and disrespectful to ask with my guest joining us at the breakfast table."

Bennet raised his mug, clearly contemplating the situation. "You know how it is, Michael, you can't keep a good stallion away from a mare when the mare's in heat."

Gabe nearly choked on his coffee. Her mother seemed mortified. Kit slammed her mug on the table despite the fact her grandmother had just walked into the dining room.

"Mr. Bennet," Gina Wheeler remarked, "my daughter is not a horse."

"I meant no disrespect. Just stating the facts the way I see them."

"Respectfully, it's time I rode on out of here," Gabe said, rising from his chair. "Thank for your hospitality, folks, and the breakfast, ma'am." He winked at Kit and touched her shoulder.

"I hope you don't think I'm being rude," Mom responded.

"Look—" Gabe said, eyeing Kit with a semblance of a smile. "I don't usually find myself in uncomfortable situations, but what happened last night needs to be worked out between Kit and myself. Frankly, there was…"

"Chemistry between us." Kit filled in the blanks, her cheeks flushing with embarrassment.

"To this day, I don't understand the periodic table and the way different elements are expected to interact together," Bennet hinted, taking a breath. "Sit down, Gabe. May I call you Gabe? I'm here to talk about horses, and if you're interested in Kit and her family situation, you might want to hear what I have to say."

"Don't take advantage of my daughter." Michael Wheeler gave a warning. "I understand she's an adult, but I don't want to see her hurt."

"This is awkward," Kit objected, sliding her chair backward from the table. "When will this family stop interfering in my life?"

"I for one would like to hear about the horses." Cole added. "Leave Kit's love life to her."

"If you're serious about racing, this family needs to start planning and training for the track," Bennet said, appearing determined. "I brought over two of my more experienced thoroughbreds. Two mares, a chestnut and a black. We need to start training. The first race takes place in Grande Prairie at the end of May."

"That's soon," Cole said. "Four weeks. Where do we look for more?"

"I've made some enquiries, but there's a rescue foundation that operates northeast of Calgary. Chance has it they have a couple thoroughbreds, but you can never tell what kind of shape they're in. It's a good place to start."

"How much money are we talking about?" Kit asked, her face still burning with embarrassment.

"You can get 'em for as low as five hundred from the rescue. Some as high as ten thousand. We'll want a healthy assortment, so you'll have to choose carefully. Don't expect we're going to win too many races, but for the sake of presentation, let's not pay any more than two or three thousand."

"And how many?"

"Sixteen head," Bennet replied. "One of you needs to round them up while I train Cole to drive and Sam to be an outrider."

Gabe sat back down at the table. Gina poured him a coffee. "Kit and I were talking last night, and I made her a proposition."

"We've heard enough talk about the affair." Sam giggled, joining them at the table with a plate of toast. Grandmother shook her head but didn't say a word. Kit glared at her little sister.

"Look. I'm not ashamed to admit that Kit and I, well, we enjoyed each other's company, hit if off from the start of the evening. But I'm not the type of man who takes advantage of anyone and I won't sit here a moment longer and…"

"Hear, hear," Bennet affirmed, raising a glass. "I like a man who doesn't shy away from responsibility or the Wheeler family. Now you were saying?"

"I want to help."

Bennet sipped his coffee. "I understand what you're trying to say, but despite the fact we appear as simple folk, we're wise to the ways of the world. And, as much as you proclaim yourself to be a gentleman, you're no more than a businessman in a suit, looking to benefit from this family's misfortune."

"Bennet, I appreciate what you're trying to say, but you're dead wrong."

"Am I, Kit?" he asked, his fingers tapping on the table. "I don't think so."

"Look, it's true. I need a proviso, a stipulation in return for my capital, but I want to help this family."

"We'll take your money," Michael Wheeler replied, pursing his lips. "We're not so proud that we won't accept your funds."

"It doesn't have to be a dirty deal. Kit and I talked. I want to sponsor the wagon with my company's brand."

"It's too late to be included in the canvas auction," Bennet stated, his face dead serious, "so we accept your offer. But let me lay it on the line for you. We'll need more than a tarp. Can you assist us financially to purchase the horses?"

"I'd like to, but I'll have to approach the TarSan board for approval."

"I suppose it's up to me to find and purchase the horses." Kit appealed to her family. "Gabe, would you be interested in coming along for the ride?"

"I feel like I'm being pushed into a situation I never planned for, but I've never been frightened away from a challenge."

"Who knew," Sam giggled, reflecting on the situation, "the bidder would get more than he bargained for."

"I've never been a man to shy away from a challenge." Gabe took a sip of coffee. "Bennet, before I leave, I'll need a rundown on the characteristics you'll require in a race horse. I imagine items such as behavioral traits, as well as age, temperament and conformation."

"Have you ridden a horse, Gabe?"

"I don't own a horse, but yes, I know how to ride."

Kit smiled at this piece of news.

Bennet looked at Kit and winked. "I like a man who knows his way around a good horse."

"Kit, I have some vacation time owing. What are you doing tomorrow?"

"No plans, Mr. Bradshaw. I'm currently on vacation."

"Miss Wheeler," he said with a straight face. "It appears we have a date to purchase horses."

"Can't wait."

"I've never seen you so happy, so free-spirited," Sam stated, laughing. "You're usually so serious. If Mr. Bradshaw is responsible for the change, you have me to thank for his timely intervention in your life."

"Well, it's been nice getting to know your family." Gabe grabbed Kit's hands and assisted her to rise from the chair, taking her arm and escorting her toward the front entrance. "Kit, it might be best if you came with me when I leave. Calgary is closer to Stirlingville."

"Not so fast," Bennet asserted. "Kit, you'll need to take my trailer and you can't have it until I unload the horses."

"No problem. Gives me time to pack a bag." She lowered her voice to a whisper. "Gabe Bradshaw, what mischief are you up to? I didn't expect to accompany you to Calgary this morning."

He leaned close and whispered in her ear. "I promised my mom I'd come over for Sunday dinner. Would you like to plead your case with my family?"

"Are they as much fun as mine?"

"Worse."

"Just let me pack a few belongings," Kit offered, biting her lip, hurrying up the stairs.

"What's going on?" Gina Wheeler called from the kitchen.

"Nothing, Mom. I'm grabbing a bag and traveling into Calgary with Gabe. Makes it easier. We'll drive to Stirlingville tomorrow. Together."

Her mom approached them. "I'm not trying to be difficult, but can I trust you with my daughter, sir?

"Absolutely, ma'am, but I won't plead my case because I'd be preaching to the choir anyway."

"I guess we understand each other then."

"We just need some time to get to know each other. I understand this is happening fast. It's happening fast for me, too."

CHAPTER 10

*K*it followed behind Gabe's BMW, driving Bennet's RAM 2500 Longhorn truck, hauling an Exiss 4H trailer. A first-born child, she'd been accustomed to hard work and operating farm machinery from a young age, and though she'd lived on the ranch for most of her life, with the exception of the time she'd been employed by Suncor, she hadn't listened to the rumble of a diesel engine in years. In her mind, an SUV was a preferred vehicle, but to pull the combined weight of a trailer loaded with horses, one needed power. She was grateful Bennet trusted her with his truck.

She maintained an even speed, driving on Highway 2 northbound, and keeping to the right-hand lane. When Calgary came in sight, she changed lanes carefully and was mindful making turns. She breathed a sigh of relief after entering the community of Evergreen.

Gabe had provided his address in case they were separated, but she hadn't experienced any difficulty and soon parked the truck and trailer in front of his house. She hated to take up space on the street and hoped the neighbors wouldn't mind.

Kit turned off the engine and glanced outside the passenger

window, scrutinizing Gabe's two-story home. Simply adorned with gray siding, and brick in tones of charcoal and beige, finding herself parked outside his residence was astounding.

Her life was changing. She could feel it. Maybe hope lingered on the horizon?

She grabbed her evening bag from the seat and stepped outside the truck, sliding to the pavement, knowing she'd be staying the night with Gabe. Was this a mistake? She didn't have time to think about it.

"Let me help you." Gabe greeted her at the curb, assisting with her bag.

Kit followed behind him as he led her to his front door. Once inside, she peered at the contemporary décor. A black leather couch, matching ottoman, and a large TV, but she only had eyes for the man.

"Nice home. How long have you lived here?"

"A little over a year. Thought it was time to move out from under my parents' wings. It was hard enough having my father manage my directives at the office. My private life needed to be, well, more private."

He gazed at her, an unmistakable look of desire in his eyes. "Are you hungry?"

Kit licked her lips and kicked off her shoes, stepping more fully into his living space. "It's only an hour or so since we ate. Right?"

"Make yourself comfortable," he offered, stepping onto a landing, gazing upward at a flight of stairs that led to a second floor. "I need to have a shower."

"Gabe?"

"Yes?"

"This is presumptuous of me. But... do you want some company? Someone to wash your back?"

He stepped down from the landing and came to her, grasping her around her waist. His fingers were warm against her hips. She peered at his earnest expression, waiting for him to speak.

"What's happening between us? It hasn't even been a week since I saw your picture in the paper. We've had a date. We've slept with each other, and now you're in my house. I'm picturing you..."

"Moving into your life? You say that as if you're concerned."

"Our relationship is maturing too fast. But it feels good having you inside my home, sharing my space. Do you know what I want right now?"

Kit stepped closer to him and leaned against his solid chest, sliding her fingers under his T-shirt, smelling his skin. He shivered beneath her touch. "I hope you'll tell me."

"Your fingers are cold."

She pressed her advantage, sliding her hand alongside his ribcage, kissing his lips. "You're hurting yourself if you don't give in to your needs. Admit you want my hands on your body."

"Oh, Kit," he moaned, grasping her hand, squeezing her fingers, and urging her to climb the stairs with him. He paused at the threshold of his bedroom. She clung to his side and stared at the untidiness, his clothing lying on the floor and the sheets on the bed, rumpled, presenting as if the man had recently crawled out and left.

"I won't apologize. This is who I am."

"A dirty boy?" Kit cooed, sliding her fingers over his crotch. "I'm not your mother."

"I see who you are. A seducer, a vixen singing a siren's song." He spun her around, devilment shining in his eyes, urging her closer to his mess. "I want to dance with you."

She swayed, willingly permitting herself to be partnered, observing an intensity in his eyes, his perusal...

"I'm not afraid. You'd never hurt me."

"By day, Kit Wheeler, I bet you give off a more wholesome image."

"It isn't yet night." She grasped his arm. "If I wasn't completely taken with you, I wouldn't consider being inside this room. I'm not investing in the physical. I didn't stand on the podium for sex."

"I didn't bid on sex, but I want it, and I want it with you."

Kit removed her jacket, letting it fall to the floor, sighing. "I'll accept you the way you are." Unbuttoning her cotton shirt, she saw how he assessed her fingers, watching the buttons escape their confinement, one after the other. "Right now, I don't care about the condition of your bed."

"What moves you, motivates your mind? What do you want from life, besides money?"

"I want you, Gabe Bradshaw." She smiled then, brazenly sliding her fingers inside his waistband, observing his Spiderman shorts rising above his jeans.

"My Spidey sense is tingling." He made known.

"Look out, here comes the Spiderman."

"I mean to," he teased, his expression acute as she undid his snap and unzipped his zipper.

"Come here, my hot little mare." He pulled her against his erection. "Your stallion awaits your pleasure."

Kit pressed closer, sliding her fingers along his ribs and the small of his back. "Come here, honey. Come and get some oats. If you're good, I'll give you an apple. You look hungry."

He growled, picked her up and carried her to his bed, placing her gently on his unmade sheets. Desirous, she squirmed as he easily removed her jeans. He permitted his own jeans to slide to the floor, then went to his knees on the bed, kissing her abdomen, breathing her scent, minding her sensitive skin until he was lapping at her sternum. When his tongue licked her silk-covered nipples, an impassioned fervor lit in her chest and heated inside her pubis, increasing her breathing.

"I'm drowning," she moaned, clutching his head, his breath fanning her neck, his mouth devouring her lips.

He chuckled in response, stopped to massage her cheekbones, the side of his thumb rhythmically sliding back and forth, staring at her eyes. "You're like an exotic flower," he breathed, scrutinizing her eyes. "A fragrance I've never smelled before."

Kit gazed at his brown eyes. "You're emotional." She realized it was true and was compelled to stroke his forehead.

"I can't believe this is happening."

She kissed his lips. "It's crazy, right?"

"Just know, my sweet little mare, once I hold a gift so special, I'll have a difficult time letting it go."

"Me, special?"

"I aim to find out."

Kit grasped Gabe's Spiderman underwear and helped him remove the boxers. Wiggling out of her pink-silk panties, she watched him fumble for a condom in the dresser drawer, then open the package with his teeth. He glanced at her. His eyes heavy with desire, he slid the rubber on his shaft.

"Come to me," she moaned, aching with need. She reclined on his bed, her head lying against his pillow.

"I want you," he breathed, his hand grasping her foot, his fingers sliding upward along her leg, drifting closer to the juncture between her thighs, his lips kissing her belly.

"Aw, darling." She squirmed, grasping his head and pulling him to her mouth.

"We'll drown together," he boasted, easing her legs apart and fitting himself between.

Kit grasped his buttocks, pulling him toward her utopia, soon gasping with the afterwaves of bliss.

Replete, they clutched each other close and drifted off to sleep. Later when Kit awoke, Gabe was resting on his elbow. He'd been watching her while she slept. He smiled, kissed her swollen lips.

"I'd like to invite you to partake of my shower. Will you come?"

Yawning, she nodded, unsuspecting of what her new lover had in mind, but once they stood in an ample shower stall with warm water cascading between their bodies, one hand stroked her inner thigh while the other clutched her breast.

"Oh, that feels good," she moaned, pressing her butt against his erection.

"And does this feel good?" he offered, stroking her labia.

"Mr. Mysterious… I had no idea…"

He turned her in the shower to face him, slipped a condom on his shaft, then positioned himself between her legs, fitting himself inside her folds, and then he began to move, again. Thrusting. Stroking. Kit groaned with the pleasure, feeling as if she might pass out from the heat. She clutched the bath rail.

Hot. Wet. Pure and unsullied physical pleasure. Kit moaned, meeting each thrust, her breath panting from her lips, her hand holding the shower rail, her mind recognizing a sense of guilt. This was sex. A woman couldn't build a long-term relationship from a physical act.

She searched Gabe's facial expression to see what he might be feeling, but his eyes were squeezed shut tight. He moaned, his face contorting with pleasure as they crossed a channel of sensuality together.

GABE FOCUSED on the road as he drove to his parents' house. He gazed at Kit sitting next to him in the passenger seat. Quiet. Contemplative. She had the look of a woman who had been thoroughly loved. Her cheeks were pink from their passion. He felt guilty for having protective thoughts, but he only wanted to turn the car around and take this woman back to his house, not sharing her with anyone. Least of all his family. Like a precious nymph washed up from the sea, he wanted to protect her and keep her close for a time.

But he'd promised his mother he'd come home for Sunday dinner.

He parked the car in the driveway, turned off the ignition and took in Kit's expression. "Are you ready for this?"

She peered through the car window, observing his family home, her expression revealing her surprise, maybe some fear, too. "Gabe,

I don't know what I was expecting to see, but your parents live in a mansion."

"I know. I lived in that house for most of my life. Look, it's a family home, no different than your ranch house. It has the same rooms as any other dwelling. The only difference is, they're bigger."

"And probably perfect, just like the manicured lawn," Kit whispered.

"I'll get your door."

Gabe opened the door to his Beamer and walked to the passenger side, soon extending his hand to Kit. When he grasped her hand, he was certain his heart skipped a beat. She looked frightened, so he squeezed her fingers.

"I'm underdressed."

"Nonsense," he said, caressing her bottom as he led her to the front door. "You look fantastic."

"A plain T-shirt and a pair of jeans. What will your family think of me?"

"At this juncture in our relationship, does it matter what my parents think? We're new. Who knows where this is going."

She frowned. But he disregarded her emotional state. He opened the front door and escorted his latest girl inside. "I'm home, Ma."

"HI, DARLING," a melodious voice echoed from somewhere inside the house. "Give me a minute. I'll be right there."

Kit stood in the entryway of the most magnificent vintage home she had ever seen, and she was sure her facial expressions registered her surprise. Oak hardwood floors shone. The upholstered furniture in the living space was pristine. A perfectly placed crystal object d'art on a silver coffee table, which was an art piece in itself. The interior was perfect, which made Kit feel inferior. She couldn't touch this life any more than she could touch the objects.

A woman sauntered forward, drying her hands on a dish towel. Long blonde hair perfectly coifed and scrutinizing brown eyes. "You've brought a guest."

"Hi Mom, I'd like you to meet Kit Wheeler."

She strolled closer, her eyes assessing. "You're the girl who Gabe placed a bid on. I thought…"

Kit didn't know what to say. Mama Bradshaw dressed her down with her eyes. She didn't welcome her into her home.

"I'm sorry, Mom. I should have told you I was bringing a girl home for dinner."

"No, no. It's okay," she said, extending her hand. "Welcome, Kit. Strange name for a girl."

"Now, Mom."

"Hmm," Kit breathed, raising her eyebrows. Surely a woman of rich means might have better manners? "It's a pet name. My real name is Katherine, but my grandmother has called me Kit since I was a young girl. Seems to have stuck and carried into my adult life. Even when I attended university, my friends called me Kit."

"That's interesting. Funny how pet names stick."

Kit didn't know what to add to the conversation. It was uncomfortable. For the space of several awkward seconds, they stared at each other. Finally, the mother gave way. "Why don't you take a seat in the living room. Would you like a drink? A glass of wine?"

Kit sighed. "Yes, please."

"White or red?"

"The lady likes green grapes, Mom. A Riesling if you have a bottle."

"I'll have Mitchell check the cellar." She nodded, then left them alone. Kit bent down and removed her leather boots. Gabe did the same.

He smiled at her in reassurance and led her to the couch. "I told you it would be rough. There isn't one girl I've brought home who hasn't faced the motherly inquisition. If it's any comfort, my mom was taken with you."

"Taken?" Kit whispered, pressing close to his ear. "Seemed to me she was ready to do battle for your innocence."

Gabe licked her ear. "I have not been innocent for a long time, but please don't tell my mother." Gabe grinned, urging her to sit beside him. He placed her hand on his thigh and kept hold of her fingers. "She's discerning; and only wants the best for her son. Give her time, she'll come around to the possibilities."

Kit didn't know what to think about the comment. She felt like she'd just met the ice queen.

"Do real people live here?" she asked.

"Definitely real."

Kit's anxiety levels climbed sitting inside the living space, likening her emotions to the stuffy airs of a museum. The rich businessman she sat beside was no more than a portrait of perfection. A Michelangelo statue, a Thomas Lawrence painting; a relationship with him amounted to an imperfect symmetry. *Damn.* They might fit together well sexually, but a relationship must be built on a stronger foundation than chemistry. Boy, Bennet was a smart man.

Gabe and Kit were from opposite walks of life. Mrs. Bradshaw could only be looking for the perfect daughter-in-law for her son. A girl who had the funds to shop at Holt Renfrew or Nordstrom's. Kit Wheeler would never measure up.

Suddenly the front door burst open and two little creatures dashed inside the house. Their faces were awash with excitement until they saw Kit sitting on the sofa. They stopped in their tracks. They retreated the way they'd come, colliding with two people who were following behind them. Dressed to the nines, a beautiful brunette wore a tan cashmere coat with a fur collar, and a handsome taller fellow, probably her husband, wore a Canada Goose down-filled luxury jacket.

They fit. They looked like they belonged here. Kit swallowed, feeling awkward in their presence. She wanted to escape. She didn't want to be here anymore.

"Mama," the little girl announced, "a stranger."

"Is that so."

She gazed around the room until their eyes met. A smile brightened her expression. "Oh, hi," she said, soon taking her daughter's coat.

"Kit, permit me to introduce my sister, Hope, her husband, Steve, and the cutest niece and nephew you'll ever meet. Tiffany and James."

The little boy held back and tucked between his mother's legs. "Say hello to Kit," Hope said, smiling.

"Hello," Tiffany replied. "Are you the lady with the horse?"

"There's a couple horses in my barn."

"I like horses."

"Maybe Miss Wheeler will let you visit her ranch sometime." Hope winked. "Then you can see her horses. I bet she'd let you stroke them."

"She'll have a few more in the barn soon," Gabe commented, squeezing Kit's fingers. "We're traveling to a rescue society tomorrow to look at two horses. Might even buy them. Maybe you could take a ride sometime."

"Not on the thoroughbreds, Gabe. They run too fast. But Molly, one of our older quarter horses, she'd be perfect. If you ever want to visit our ranch, that is."

Hope passed her coat to her husband and approached Kit where she sat on the couch, taking a seat on the opposite sofa. She must have noticed her discomfort.

"It's a lot to take in, but don't worry. We're much the same as other families. We have our wrinkles and our warts, and all these wrappings." She pointed to a painting above the fireplace. "But they hide the imperfections. Underneath it all, we're human. Just like you."

"You're perceptive," Kit said, breathing again.

Gabe laughed. "There's actually a big hole behind the Claude Monet painting."

Mitchell Bradshaw walked into the room just then carrying

James. Tiffany sat beside her mother. "Gabe should know since he's the rascal who put the hole in the wall." He gave his son a commanding stare.

"Perhaps save the story for another day." Gabe winced, glancing at Kit. "I don't want to scare off my guest. Dad, I'd like you to meet Kit Wheeler."

Kit rose from the sofa and accepted his father's handshake. His steel-gray eyes were not any less intense than his wife's, but he softened the look with a measured curiosity.

"So, you're the woman who was featured in the Herald, who has captured the interest of my son."

Kit glanced at Gabe momentarily, then back at his father. "I'm not sure how to respond. I'm grateful for Gabe's help. My family can cover two mortgage payments with his bid."

"I don't like the pursuit of the wagon part. Isn't racing adding further risk to the financial situation? I don't like risk in my business."

"Well," Kit said, becoming emotional, "it seemed like a good plan when we first discussed the idea as a family. And, it's our heritage. Our grandfather's legacy."

"Dad," Gabe appealed, his voice taking an edge. "I don't think it's your place to advise the Wheeler family on their life choices."

Mitchell sat on a nearby armchair and placed his grandson on his lap. "TarSan Oil financed the date, right? A date lasting more than one evening, more than one day?"

Kit took a deep breath. "Mr. Bradshaw, if you were not sincere in wanting to help my family…"

"Let's be clear, it was my son who was attracted to your story."

Kit glanced at Gabe, seeing concern mar his features. She rose from the couch. "I'm sorry to have intruded on your family dinner. She pulled out her cell phone as she made her way to the front entrance. "Please excuse me."

"Wait a minute, Kit," Gabe called after her, rising from the sofa.

"Enjoy your dinner with your family," Kit replied, sliding her feet into her leather boots, her breath puffing from between her lips. "I'll find my own way home."

"Don't leave."

"What's happening?" Gabe's mother asked, coming to the front door.

Kit ignored the comment and grasped his arm, trying to squash the tears building behind her eyes. "If I didn't know it before, I know now. I don't belong here in this museum, and that means I don't belong with you."

"Dad, what have you done?" she heard his sister say as she passed through the doorway, not bothering to shut the heavy oak door.

She rushed down the driveway, striding past a perfectly manicured lawn, with tension exploding in her chest, constricting her breathing. She took a shuddering breath, tears collecting in her eyes, making it difficult to see. She swiped them away.

"Hold up, Kit," she heard Gabe call after her. She heard his footfalls, then felt hands on her shoulders as he grasped her, soon turning her to meet his concerned expression.

"Oh darling," he said, appearing concerned, "please don't cry. My father didn't mean to upset you. Come back inside."

"I don't think so, Gabe. I don't belong here. I want to go home."

"They're agreeable when you get to know them. Honestly, they are…" He wiped the tears from her eyes. His thumb pad caressing her cheeks. "I warned you, it wouldn't be easy."

Kit glanced at the front doorway, seeing his mother and father standing at the entrance. What did it mean? Suddenly, Mama Bradshaw hurried outside, carrying a crystal goblet in her hands.

"My husband can be blunt," she said, taking a breath, "but he didn't mean to offend you. Please accept our apologies and come back inside. My son will never forgive us if you don't. I brought you a glass of wine as a peace offering."

Kit didn't know what to do. "She's right," Gabe said, grasping her hand. "Please?"

Kit silently nodded, relenting quicker than she thought was wise and then followed Gabe back inside the house. Little Tiffany ran to meet her and grasped her hand, leading her back to the couch. "Grandpa is mean," she said, sitting beside her. "Grandpa, don't you ruin my chance to ride a real horse."

"Dad's a hard ass," Hope said, supporting her daughter. "But he's a good guy, Kit. He didn't mean to upset you."

Kit took a deep breath and wiped another tear away. She studied the people staring at her, assessing mother and father, a sister and her husband, and finally Gabe, hoping for courage to say what needed to be said.

"I want you to know that regardless of what journalists write, my family's plight is real. We're fighting to save our ranch. A plot of land has belonged to the Wheelers for over fifty years. A wagon represents our way of life and to save our farm, we have to ride the half mile of Baby Blue. It was my sister's idea. My brother Cole is excited and my father, the gambler, the one partly responsible for this situation, is excited, too."

Kit took a deep breath, then sipped her wine. It was good. "Frankly, I've never been down this road. I was a project manager for Suncor, so I have some knowledge in leading a team, but am I doing what's right? I honestly don't know."

"We're putting the tarp on their wagon, aren't we, Dad?"

"If I didn't know your situation before, Kit, I understand it better now. If you need legal support, we can help you."

"Really?"

"Look, it's time our company helped a family, just like Gabe has been urging me to do. Patti, will you bring the glasses?"

"Just so you know," Kit said earnestly, willing the tears not to fall. "I appreciate your support and thank you for offering it. The least we can do is have you to the ranch and let Tiffany ride Molly."

Tiffany clapped her hands. Her little face lit the room with joy.

Soon everyone had a glass of wine in their hands and were clinking cheers. If tears were the means to usher in compassion and release suspicion, Kit was grateful for her bout of emotion, but emotion wouldn't assist a family with winning the race. They still had miles to go and a family dinner to get through.

CHAPTER 11

*L*ife progressed faster as one aged. If Dot blinked, she'd miss the passing days. The sun slipped beneath the horizon quicker, and most days she'd barely laid her head on the pillow, closing her eyes, only to open them again to the sun coming around again. Older. Wiser. If only her family appreciated their grandmother's wisdom.

The days passed as if no one was paying attention. No one listened to her anyway, so she had stopped telling them what to do. Conversations only ended in conflict. She didn't like it. Hated it even. She was too old for this nonsense.

Dot Wheeler struggled with the apprehension, her heart filling with sorrow, discomfort, and worry as she walked toward the barn. She needed to take action, but what steps might end this madness? What could she do? What could an old woman do? She loved her family and would do anything to protect them, even if it meant destroying the wagon.

Baby Blue. Dangerous wagon. Why had John named it after her?

At age seventy-seven, her soul was heavy in her body. Everything hurt. Her knees ached as she ambled forward beside the fence line, but she still enjoyed the crunching sound of her boots against the rocks. Some motions still carried weight. She made her way along the road, alone, glimpsing the slight impression of tracks where the wagon used to run, but even in the twilight hours with the sun slipping beneath the horizon, she could still glimpse the old impression.

Damn. Right there, obvious if you knew what to look for, just like the wagon. She shook her head with the weight of the burden squeezing her heart. Why hadn't she rid herself of that wagon? Baby Blue, parked in front of the barn.

It didn't matter that the beast was refreshed with paint, it was still the weapon that had carried her husband to his death. She stopped in front of the old cart, refusing to touch the wooden frame, but scrutinizing the old box, her mouth pinching, remembering... hearing the horn blow, seeing the outrider, seeing Bennet, throwing the stove into the back of the wagon.

"And they're off..." the announcer had cried.

She closed her eyes, recalling the weight of exhilaration, of cheering fans, screaming fans in the stands, bursting to life in her mind. And the terror and exhilaration John had once loved: Baby Blue taking to the inside rail, the horses' heads stretching forward, their hooves pounding against the earth, exploding along the half mile of Hell, *and her husband*, wearing his determined expression, his hands that had once held hers slapping the reins on the horses' backs as he drove his thoroughbreds forward. *Hah!*

The emotion built. Dot sucked in a breath and a tear slipped from her eye. She wiped the emotion away. More anger than sadness. So many years had slipped by and she missed her husband still. Had loved him as much as she loved their child, Michael, and the blessings of family who had come after him to share this ranch with her.

She wouldn't see any harm come to them. She had to take action. Soon.

"Dot," a familiar voice called to her, "how come you're here all alone?"

"Just remembering." She turned to face Bennet. "I thought you had left?"

"I did. I came back. I wanted to talk to you. In private."

"Why did you do it, Bennet? Why did you offer to help train? Now you have Kit searching for horses. Cole riding the wagon and Sam aiming to take your position as an outrider. Isn't it enough I lost John? Why are you doing this to me?"

"Sweetheart..."

"Don't call me that."

"Look, whether you like it or not, it's the right step to take."

She gazed at him, seeing his gentleness, his attempt at understanding, but also a firmness. She felt betrayed. "How is it right to take my adult children on a journey that once robbed me of their father, their grandfather?"

"Dot, I've told you this before. You must overcome your grief. You've carried this burden, this anger, for over fifty years. Most of your young life. Let it go."

She didn't reply. She turned away from him, but he wasn't finished.

"When will you let the best of your husband shine through? John loved this sport. Yes, the race comes with risk, but how can life be enjoyed if one never takes a leap of faith? John loved his sport as much as he loved you. His family recognizes and celebrates their grandfather's past. You cannot keep their heritage from them any longer."

"Heritage? Legacies are not built on the race track. I don't want to see another family member injured, or God forbid..."

"Frankly, it upsets me that you've hidden John's truth, buried his memory in the barn with the wagon. I'm glad Kit unearthed Baby Blue."

"You don't see what I see."

"You're right. I don't. I've looked past the accident. You should have seen Cole's eyes today as he came around the bend in the track. Brought tears to my eyes. Cole couldn't understand why an old man was smiling. Hell, crying."

"'Cause you're an old fool."

He stepped forward and grasped her old wrinkled hands, squeezing her fingers. She let him. "An old fool who loves you, Dorothy Wheeler. I'm too old to sneak inside your house through the bedroom window. I want to share my life with you now that my wife is gone. It's time to tell your children. My children, too."

"You're right." Dot leaned against Bennet's chest, glad to have his strength, his wisdom. But she wasn't ready to see the past his way.

"Sweetheart, you understand what I'm trying to say, right?"

"You've made your point," Dot stated, taking a deep breath. "We'll tell them at the next family dinner."

"I'm glad you see this my way. It's time to embrace the future."

There was no use in arguing with Bennet. A man needed to know he was right. A woman? A woman needed to do only what was necessary to protect her family.

CHAPTER 12

*G*abe and Kit had been traveling north on the Queen Elizabeth II Highway, heading for Stirlingville, Alberta. They exited the main highway and merged onto 581 East. According to the GPS, they were close to the Equine Rescue Society. Kit slowed the Ram truck to a crawl, watching for the side road that would lead them to the property.

"There's the signage." Gabe pointed. "Looks like we've arrived."

Kit turned left, then drove along a narrow gravel roadway lined with poplar trees and thick bushes on the right, and verdant-green pastures on the left. Kit glanced at the horses grazing.

"There must be at least fifty head."

"They're beautiful," Gabe replied, stretching forward, his hand on the dashboard. "Wow. One doesn't see that many horses in a field anymore. They paint a pretty picture."

"They're the embodiment of fine art. Majestic beauties."

Chestnuts and dark browns, a few bays, and the odd black beauty and spotted gray in the mix. Kit couldn't read the mind of a horse but if she could, she'd have to say these equines seemed happy. She paused the vehicle to watch them and observed their easy manner, the tilt of their heads and the swish of their tails.

Their casual interest in the truck and trailer passing by, then back to grazing.

"These horses are fortunate," Kit stated, frowning. "Thanks to the generosity and commitment from people like Margaret Green, they've been rescued from terrible situations. Abuse, neglect, even slaughter."

"I'm sure there's any number of reasons why horses end up in places like this," Gabe said, his eyebrows rising.

"True enough," Kit replied, pressing on the gas and moving forward again. "But now that I'm here, I'm more mindful of the situations that bring horses to a rescue society. Terrible situations. Kind of pulls at my heartstrings."

"Honestly," Gabe said, placing his hand on her thigh. "I had no idea. I hope we can save a few of these horses."

"We?" Kit smiled.

Gabe merely winked at her in response.

Kit drove farther along the gravel road and soon parked the truck and trailer by the fence line, near a simple white bungalow. She put the truck in park and turned off the ignition. "I can't wait to see them."

"I've done a lot of stuff in my life," Gabe said, opening his door and stepping to the ground. "Can't say I've ever been part of a rescue operation before. Kind of feels good."

He came around to her side of the truck and opened her door. Kit accepted his grasp, his fingers cold against her palm. "None of this would be possible without you. Frankly, Gabe, I can't believe you're here with me."

He pulled her into his arms. The intensity of his nut-brown eyes and the passion she saw shining in their depths, squeezed at her heart, making it difficult to breathe. Could a woman fall in love so fast? This man would be easy to love.

"That makes two of us. Let's meet Marg and see what her rescue operation is all about."

They walked toward the farmhouse, but the woman who Kit

had talked to on the phone must have seen them parking their vehicle. She exited the house and approached them. She was a stocky woman and Kit could tell straight away she was kind. She waved a greeting, smiling. Short silver hair streaked with gray framed a weather-worn face, and when she smiled, pleasant wrinkles settled in the corners of her slate-gray eyes. A distinct mien had Kit wondering. A sentiment she couldn't explain as Margaret Green scrutinized her guests.

"Howdy," she called, extending her hand. "I'm Margaret Green, but please call me Marg. You must be Kit. And this is Gabe? Is that right?"

"Yes," Gabe said, "a pleasure to meet you, ma'am."

"How was the drive from Calgary?"

"Good," Kit replied. "We made good time."

"Well, I'm glad you arrived safely. So, Bennet tells me you're in the market for some horses."

"Yes. I'm not sure if you've heard much about the Wheeler family. We've been in the news recently."

"Can't say I have." She placed her thumbs in the loops of her jeans. "I don't have much time for watching television with fifty or so head of horses. I spend my days rehabilitating and rehoming these majestic creatures."

Kit studied Margaret. She wore a pale-blue Western shirt with a down-filled navy vest and blue jeans. Nothing fancy. "We have a specific need. We're looking to purchase approximately fifteen horses, thoroughbreds mostly, to pull a chuckwagon."

Margaret pulled a packet of cinnamon gum from her jeans pocket. "Want one?"

"No, thank you," Kit said with surprise, glancing at Gabe.

She unwrapped the chewing gum, assessing them the entire time, then finally popped the stick in her mouth and chewed. Kit swore the purpose of the exercise was to scrutinize her guests.

"I have a few that might work, but as I told Bennet, they'll require a lot of hard work and training. And that's *if*," she emphasized, kicking at a speck of dirt on the ground, "if I deem you responsible enough to purchase them in the first place. Would you like to see them?"

"Yes," Kit replied, suddenly nervous.

"Some are in the field. We'd have to catch them," she said, laughing. "Did you bring some carrots? An apple?"

"Never thought about it, actually."

"That's okay, I have plenty," she noted, walking away. "Come. I've placed two mares in the barn. You'll love these girls. They're special."

"Can you tell me about your operation?" Kit asked, following a step behind.

"Well, we've been in business for four years," she said, gazing back, as if appraising the potential buyers. "My husband and I have always had a passion for horses. We're retired but became concerned about the high number of horses being auctioned off to slaughter. Good horses. Horses in their prime. Yearlings. Mares with foals. Or horses, frankly, that people don't want anymore. I appealed to my husband with these old eyes, and we were soon in the business of saving horses."

"Where do your horses come from?"

"Many come from auctions. Some from feedlots. We're kind of like the SPCA, except for horses. If someone for any reason can't take care of their horse, we don't ask questions. We take the animal into our care."

"Where do the thoroughbreds come from?"

"Does it matter? Almost all our horses were in a terrible situation and needed help," she replied, pausing at the barn door. She slid large wooden panels aside, then paused at the threshold. Her hand on the wood. "Look, some of these animals have had a tough life, so the folks at the rescue like to ensure they get a good home. So, we don't just adopt our animals out to anyone. Suppose I decide you're a good candidate to adopt one of our rescues, only then will we talk about you taking one home."

"What are you saying?" Gabe asked.

"I'm telling you, I'll answer your questions, but I expect answers in return. I don't mean to disparage your interest in our operation, but The Equine Rescue Society is searching for responsible owner-ship, forever homes for our animals. We need to ensure whoever adopts our horses can care for them for a lifetime."

Kit thought about Marg's comment and considered her family's financial situation. Maybe her grandmother was right. If they were not able to save the farm, what would happen to the horses?

"Miss Wheeler," Marg asked, staring. "Can you provide a forever home for any of these animals?"

Kit swallowed; she didn't know what to say.

"Yes, she can," Gabe replied with some seriousness, perhaps trying to offer his reassurance. "Kit and I are in this together. We will take care of any horses we adopt."

She assessed them. "You two a couple? I don't see a ring on this gal's finger."

"Well," Kit said, gazing at the ground, "the truth is…"

Gabe grasped her shoulder and pulled her close to him. "What Kit is trying to say, is that we have not known each other for long, so she hasn't said yes, not yet. But we are a couple."

"We are?" Kit questioned, her eyebrows rising.

"You know we are, honey."

"There's definitely sparks flying between the two of you. I like sparks." Marg grinned, stepping farther inside the barn, "as long as they don't ignite my hay. Come on in. Let's meet Jewel and her foal, Pepper."

Kit was surprised when Gabe reached for her hand. Smiling, he squeezed her fingers as they followed Marg into the barn. They didn't have far to go.

"This is Jewel." Marg stroked a gray horse's muzzle. The horse nickered and nodded its head as if it understood what her owner was saying. "Jewel came from a feedlot. She and her foal were purchased for meat."

"Her foal?"

"That's right, she has a young 'un. She's a thoroughbred, and I know you weren't thinking of a mare with a foal. She's a good horse."

Kit stepped forward, gazing into the animal's dark eyes. She felt its warmth as it snorted, neighing, pawing the ground. She reached for the muzzle and let the animal smell her hand. "She's absolutely beautiful."

"Yes, she is."

"May we go inside the stall?" Gabe asked. "Check her conformation."

"You're more likely to get a hoof up the rear end," she chuckled, chewing. "Never can tell how a horse might react to strangers, especially when she has a newborn foal. Why don't the two of you go back outside. I'll put a bridle on her and bring her out."

"Sure," Kit agreed.

Gabe, still holding her hand, escorted her outside.

"You wouldn't know it by looking at the woman, but she's a tough old bird."

"One who takes her job seriously. I admire her values."

Shortly thereafter, Marg led Jewel to where they stood, and a tiny spotted foal followed behind its mother. The young horse was clumsy on its legs. The mother raised its head and nickered loudly, prancing backward on its hooves.

"Whoa, girl," Marg soothed, completely in control.

Kit stepped forward, letting go of Gabe's hand.

"Just give her some time to get used to you," Marg implored.

"So, clearly Jewel is a beautiful horse." Gabe stepped forward to ponder the horse. "But given that she has a foal, she can't be in peak condition. I can't say I know a ton about horses, but I can't imagine using her on the track."

"It's true. Most drivers wouldn't use a mare who has foaled, but some girls continue to race when they're able, returning to their abilities, so to speak."

"She must be at least sixteen hands high," Kit said, patting her neck. "I absolutely adore her."

"It's too bad we can't purchase her."

"Why not?" Kit asked, gazing at Gabe with her forehead furrowed.

"You heard what Marg said. She's not in peak condition. You need horses that will give you a chance at winning."

"I suppose you're right," Kit sighed, wishing it were not so. "Marg, do you have any other thoroughbreds?"

"Yes, but they're roaming in the pasture. Are you okay walking among the horses?"

"Yes."

"Let me put Jewel back in the stable."

SHORTLY THEREAFTER, Kit and Gabe followed Marg as she led them in the direction of their truck, soon taking them to a gate. They entered a pass-through Y-gate, maneuvering around the triangular bend, and coming into the pasture on the other side. They sighted the horses they had seen before. The group of equines looked at them, tails swishing. A lead horse clearly understood three humans were strolling across their pasture and coming closer to him. Head high and ears raised tall, the dark-brown horse trotted forward a few paces, then paused, watching them come.

"That's Barron," Marg said, strolling forward. "He's the leader of the herd. He's my favorite. I'll never part with him. Just watch, he'll come to me. He knows his master and I bet he can already smell the apple in my pocket."

And Marg was right. When they came within a few feet, Barron trotted forward. "He'll be curious about you." She patted his neck. Kit watched as the horse pushed its head into Marg's hand, nickering.

"Oh, all right," Marg gushed, retrieving the apple. A few other horses seemed curious about what was happening and wandered closer.

"Where are the thoroughbreds?" Gabe asked.

"The two chestnut mares, the bay, and the pretty little gray over there." She pointed, then turned to face them.

"Why were you in the news?" she asked, seemingly out of the blue.

Kit didn't know what to say. She looked at Gabe in appeal, went to reply, but didn't know how to respond. Panic suffused her cheeks with red.

"Do you want to tell me what's going on here?"

Kit took a deep breath. "My family has been down on their luck. Our ranch was threatened with foreclosure. It's a long story, but…"

"Maybe we should go back to the house and talk about it."

Margaret Green began walking, leading them back across the pasture with her horse, Barron, following close behind. Kit had to hurry to keep up with her stride. "Please don't think badly of me."

She glanced her way, clearly assessing. "It's odd is all, that a financially strapped family would want to adopt horses. If you can't pay your bills, how will you feed them?"

"I'm here to help," Gabe said, eyeing Kit.

Kit raised her hands in exasperation. "A news story shared the plight of our family, and the fact that my grandfather used to race."

"I knew your grandfather," she pointed out, keeping her stride. "He was a good man."

"You knew my grandfather?"

"John took better care of his horses than his wife. I can't imagine your grandmother is in favor of your desire to race."

"She isn't."

Marg paused, and glanced back. "You must have a good reason then, to go against your grandmother's wishes, and take the risk."

"Yes," Kit explained, sighing. "The Wheeler family has pledged to enter the circuit. The Grand Prairie Stompede begins in four weeks. We need Baby Blue to cross the finish line. If by chance we're among the eight fastest teams, we'll make it to the Calgary Stampede, if we win the race."

Marg shook her head. "You're no different than your grandfather."

Kit grasped Marg's hand. "We're sunk if you don't let us adopt."

"Join me at the house. I need to think about this."

~

THEY WERE SOON SEATED at Marg's kitchen table, drinking coffee. Kit observed that Marg hadn't bothered to remove her boots, and the messy and disorganized house stunk of horse. Dirty dishes were piled in the sink. Apparently, Marg took better care of her horses than her humble home.

She took a sip of her coffee, and then placed her mug on the table. "I will risk selling my horses to you, if Mr. Bradshaw gives his solemn vow he'll help manage the horses."

"I promise to do my best," Gabe said, glancing at Kit. "We're grateful. But why?"

"Every horse comes to the rescue with some problem or another and requires help and training to overcome the abuse they may have suffered."

"How does your treatment of horses relate to my family's situation?"

"Your family has a lot to overcome. I know you think the race might be the answer, but what if you lose? What if the Stampede board doesn't invite you to the Calgary Stampede?"

"I won't think about that right now."

"I'd be lying if I didn't tell you that it's next to impossible you'll win the race with my horses."

"Why would you discourage us?"

"They're not in peak condition. Overweight, too skinny, or behavioral issues—the horses won't be prepared to race in three weeks. Sure, they'll run. They're spirited animals. But they'll never be able to compete against champion drivers and horses that cost thousands of dollars."

"No hope at all?" Gabe asked, witnessing Kit's facial expression fall, deflating like a balloon losing air.

Marg gave her a half-smile. "Sure, there's always the horse that surprises. Happens all the time, and people love cheering for the underdog, don't they, but it's more likely you'll come in dead last. I want you to understand what you're facing should you agree to adopt my horses."

"It's pretty clear." Kit sighed. "Thank you for explaining the pitfalls. Can we take the four thoroughbreds when we leave today?"

"You're as single-minded as your grandfather before you."

"My family is determined to see this race through to the end."

"Well, I tell you what. I like that kind of determination. We'll talk about a fee. I'll explain the adoption process, which will include a few visitations to ensure the horses are adapting to their new home. If this is agreeable, my husband and I will round up the horses and help load them inside your trailer. Are you sure you're up to this?"

"Yes." Kit and Gabe agreed at the same time.

"Okay, then," Marg exclaimed, downing her coffee and rising from the table. "Let's go get your horses."

"Why are you trusting us with them?" Kit asked.

"The risk is acceptable, and with the money your boyfriend pays me, I'll be able to rescue more horses. And helping equines is my mission."

CHAPTER 13

$\mathcal{K}$it leaned against the passenger door of the truck, setting her sights on wheat fields, round hay bales, and homesteads with barns all too often painted red. In the background, the radio played a favorite song by Mumford & Sons. Kit loved the twang of the banjo, the pounding beat of the drum and the keening cry of the lead singer: "*and I'll kneel down—*"

She glanced at Gabe Bradshaw. Sparks had ignited into flames. She hoped for a forever devotion and a man who might pledge his hand and hold her dear for the rest of their lives. She was thirty years old; the clock was ticking. Was he the one?

Gabe had insisted on driving back to the ranch and she had to admit, it felt good having him in her life. A hub for her wheel, a foundation to support her everyday needs, a partner to share the burdens and assist in shaping her new world. This change in her life was too good to be true.

He glanced at her and she smiled, wondering if he could read her mind. That look. This connection. The bridge spanning a space she couldn't see nudged her breastbone and quickened her breathing. She swallowed, studying his eyes, his leather coat, his striped cotton shirt with a white collar escaping his leather jacket. The top

116

two buttons were undone. She wanted to draw her fingers along the neckline, undoing the remaining buttons to touch his skin.

"What are you looking at, beautiful?"

"You," she confessed.

"Come on over here, slide next to me."

Kit didn't hesitate. She unfastened her seat belt, knowing it was unwise, and then shifted into the middle and refastened the belt. He placed his hand on her thigh and a thrill of excitement surged in her female parts. "Gabe, did you mean what you said to Margaret? That we were a couple?"

He stared at the road ahead, clearly thinking. Finally, he gripped her leg with his fingers. "You know, I don't touch just anyone's thigh," he said, smiling, "for that matter, it's not the usual circumstance for me to fall into any woman's bed."

Kit touched his hand, sighing, sliding her fingers easily over his knuckles. "I don't know where our relationship is going, but I sure enjoy sitting beside you."

"The feeling's mutual."

"Do you still have the paper? The one with my portrait?"

"I wouldn't part with it. I'll ask your little sister for the original image. It's a keeper."

"Gabe, I know the paper led you to me, but it's not my best photograph."

"Honey, that picture's worth a million bucks."

"Why?"

"It led me to you."

"All the same…"

"Just let it be, darling. I see the questioning look in your eyes. Let's not pressure ourselves to kneel just yet. Permit our relationship to take its course and develop naturally."

"I'm thirty, Gabe."

"Over the hill." He winked, licking his lips. "But the filly can still swish her tail and the stallion can smell the honey."

Kit broke out in laughter. "I'm not a mare, Gabe Bradshaw. You

117

need to spend more time on a ranch. It's more like the girl can still run and the stallion, well, he can give chase."

He glanced out the window, then at the road ahead. "Court actually, but I can smell your perfume."

"Baby Rose Jeans. My mother gave it to me."

He grinned, squeezed her leg again. "The scent of fresh powder with notes of citrus. I'm hungry for an orange."

"A perfume connoisseur? You surprise me. Why are you single? A man like you should have been married a long time ago."

"Everything in its own time. Seriously," he said, his eyes so desirous her breath caught in her throat, "I've been waiting for my soulmate."

"Do you think you've found her? My ovaries are crying for a release that might benefit mankind."

Grinning, he gazed at the road ahead after her comment, obviously contemplating. Together, they watched a truck and trailer drive past on the opposite side of the road.

"Someone's always moving something. I could see myself planting seeds, planting a birthright, with someone like you."

"You're avoiding my comment."

"Honey, I'm not avoiding what's happening between us."

He drew his finger along the inside of her thigh and came dangerously close to her erogenous zone. She sucked in a breath. Surprised.

"Just so happens, I've have been searching for a safe haven myself. I'm thirty-four. I want children, too. Is that what you were suggesting?"

"Might have been."

"I could give them to you, whether you marry me or not."

Kit heated, laughing aloud to disguise her anxiety, then grabbed his hand and placed it back on the steering wheel. "Just a few more miles to go. Let's get the horses to the ranch safely."

"I'll stay the night if you invite me."

"You'll have to." Kit giggled, thinking she was funny. "You're trapped here without your BMW."

"It's clever maneuvering, either way," he said with a grin, his smile as infectious as his humor. "You'll have to drive me home."

$\sim$

GABE PARKED the truck and trailer near the pasture's gate. Kit didn't think it odd that Baby Blue wasn't parked near the barn, as she knew Bennet had been mentoring her brother on the track.

Kit jumped from the truck. "I'll find Cole. We'll need his help off-loading the horses."

"I'll wait here."

Kit walked toward the house but turned back, taking in the trailer and the barn. She shook her head and made her way across the gravel walkway. She climbed the few stairs to the porch and passed through the doorway. She removed her boots and then walked to the kitchen, hearing steam whistling from the kettle.

All smiles, her grandmother was pouring boiling water into a mug.

"Hi, Gran. Have you seen Cole?"

She glanced her way, then back at her cup. "Bennet picked him up. Something about a friend with some horses."

"Oh. Gabe and I transported four horses from the rescue. He's waiting outside. I was hoping Cole could help us unload them. Is Dad around?"

"He had an errand to run for me. My eye medicine was running low. He's gone into town to refill the prescription."

"My sister?"

"Her bidder came by to take her on their date."

"Yes, that's right. I'd forgotten about her date. What am I to do?" Kit asked, scrutinizing her grandmother's happy expression. "Gabe doesn't have enough experience to unload the horses and Mom will be no use."

"No. She's afraid of larger animals. Won't even go near the cows."

Kit took a step closer to her grandmother, suddenly curious. "Gran, you seem preoccupied. Is there something I should know?"

Quiet, she took a seat at the table. She calmly placed a tea bag into her cup, then glanced out the window.

"I suppose I'll have to tell you."

Her grandmother scrutinized Kit with a look that caused shivers to tickle her spine. A self-assured smug expression. "What have you done, Gran?"

"I've sold Baby Blue. You might as well take those horses back where you brought them from. The racing is over."

"You what?"

"You heard me."

Kit fell into the chair across from her grandmother, disbelieving. But she'd seen for herself, the wagon was gone. And then a memory, a vehicle pulling a trailer…

Suddenly angry, she rose upward. "How could you?"

"You," Gran exclaimed, her voice turning harsh, "had no right to bring that wagon into the light of day."

Kit tried to remain calm. She didn't want to upset her grandmother, but she needed to press. "Gran, you don't understand."

"I'm old but not dumb. I should have sold that wagon years ago."

A pain erupted in Kit's chest, her legs felt weak. She grabbed her head just as Gabe appeared inside the house. He walked into the kitchen and took one look at her face and…

"You might as well know, I sold the wagon. No one will be hurt now. It's gone."

"We'll be laughingstocks," Kit moaned, staring at her grandmother, and then Gabe. "After all the media attention and taking the wagon back to the track. What will people think of us?"

"I'll buy it back," Gabe pledged, his hands on his hips.

Grandmother merely laughed, shaking her head, but the

somber tone of her voice wasn't funny. "No, you won't. You'll never find it."

"Kit. The vehicle we passed, the one on the highway with the trailer…"

"The wagon must have been beneath the canvas."

"We need to convene an emergency meeting. Send a text to your family. Come Hell or high water, we'll find Baby Blue."

CHAPTER 14

"Gall darn it," Bennet grumbled, downing a shot of whiskey, "I should have seen this coming."

Kit watched their family friend pacing back and forth in front of the fireplace, stomping the fibers of the living room rug. He hadn't even bothered to remove his cowboy hat. If he didn't calm himself soon, he'd wear a hole in the carpet, or worse, have a heart attack.

"How could you have known?" Michael Wheeler replied, reaching for the Crown Royal and taking a swig, not bothering for a liquor glass. "No one can read my mother's mind. She does what she wants. Always has and always will."

"Michael!" Gina scolded, sitting on the sofa beside her husband. "Don't be unkind. Mom is in the room. She's listening to every word you say. Now, I don't understand why this is happening, but I'm sure Mom has her reasons for parting with Baby Blue."

"She sold the wagon. Right out from under us." Cole ranted, anger furrowing his forehead. "What kind of an ignorant move was that?" Kit had never seen her brother so angry. His face was bright red.

"Now, now, son," Bennet remarked, pointing a finger. "I won't hear any aggressive talk against your grandmother."

Kit glanced at her Gran to see if the comment upset her. Her eyebrows rose in interest, but she kept rocking in her chair, swaying back and forth. In the face of her family's anger, Kit was surprised she could be so calm, but she had raised a son. She'd taken care of her boy and this ranch for most of her life. She'd learned a long time ago how to manage a family.

"Who are you to tell me how to talk to my Gran," Cole howled, fuming.

"I'll tell you who I am…"

Shaking her head, Dot raised her hand in appeal, pausing in her motion. "Mind your manners, grandson. This man has been sweet on me since the day John died. Seems like it's as good a time as any to tell the family. Bennet?"

"We've been seeing each other since Betsey passed away."

No one seemed surprised. Kit shook her head. Cole rolled his eyes. Samantha was furious. "This was my date night. Does anyone know what I've gone through to try and support this family? And once again, you go and ruin everything. Gran, I think everyone knows you care about Bennet, but if you wanted to get rid of the wagon, why couldn't you have waited one more night?"

Kit glanced at Sam's date. An Asian man, he appeared uncomfortable, but who wouldn't be when thrust into the middle of a family drama. She noticed he kept glancing at Gabe.

"Do you two know each other?" Kit asked, curious.

"Well…" Sam's date muttered.

"You do!" Kit retorted, emphasizing her surprise. "How can you possibly know each other?"

"Everyone, this is Jared," Gabe admitted, shaking his head. "Jared is my public relations expert at TarSan Oil."

"Your what?"

"Now, Kit, before you get angry or think a conspiracy is taking place, I had no idea Jared had placed a bid on Sam."

"How could you not have known?"

"As I recall, during the time of the bidding, I was with you."

"What does it matter who he works for," Sam persisted, rising from her chair, "this was my date night!"

"Who the H-E-double-hockey-sticks cares about you and your date," Cole growled. "We have bigger issues to discuss than your social affairs. There's only one subject that matters. Where's the chuckwagon?" He pleaded, raising his hands. "We have to get it back. We can't train for the race without it!"

Kit frowned seeing how Cole's comment made her grand-mother smirk. "Cole is right. Finding the wagon is all that matters. Gran, please tell us, where did Baby Blue go?"

That same pinched expression returned to Dot's face. She glanced at her family as if considering how to reply, but then carried on rocking, choosing to remain silent.

Sam threw up her hands in exasperation.

"Come on, Mother." Michael tried to negotiate. "Where did you send the wagon?"

Dot Wheeler rose from her rocking chair, placed her hands on her hips and glared at her son. She had a few first-class expressions for the rest of her family, too.

"You can pry all you want. You can accuse me and berate me until the cows come home, but you're not getting so much as a piece of cherry pie from my kitchen cupboards. The wagon is gone. It's not coming back. Live with it!"

"We can figure this out," Cole said, scratching his head. "How many people does Gran know for heaven's sake? In the village of Longview, we're surrounded by a small community of peers."

"Good call," Michael Wheeler concurred. "Clearly, your grand-mother will not tell us anything. However, she must have sold the wagon to someone. Maybe someone she knows?"

Kit threw her hands up in exasperation, thinking aloud. "A friend? A neighbor?"

"The church?" Gina ruminated, gazing at her husband.

"The 4-H Club?" Cole added.

"The bank?" Gabe offered, shaking his head. "If I were your grandmother, that's where I'd send the wagon."

Grandmother went white. She returned to her rocking chair.

"Dot," Bennet said, coming to stand beside his sweetheart, "does the money lender have the wagon?"

She puffed a big sigh. "It was the proper step to take. We owe money on this property and the bank holds the mortgage."

"How much did you get, if you don't mind me asking?"

"Two hundred dollars."

"Ah…" Sam complained as if someone had punched her in the gut. "It's worth far more than that. They've robbed us."

"It's a fair price, considering they had to pick it up."

"How will we get it back?" Kit asked, rising from the couch.

"You won't."

Grandmother wore a satisfied grin. Kit shouldn't be surprised, but she was. Her Gran was bold and shouldn't have been discounted. She could see the truth now.

Michael Wheeler shook his head. "Why did you do this, Mom?"

"No one will listen to me!" Gran shouted. "The wagon doesn't belong to you. I have expressed my feelings, time and time again. I told you I didn't want this family to race. You went against my wishes. I will keep my family safe!"

The room went silent while everyone thought about a grandmother's accusations.

Cole sulked like a little boy whose toy had been stolen. Kit could tell how much this race, this journey, meant to him.

"Gran—" Kit pleaded, trying to see the situation no different than her grandmother, "—why does this bother you so much? Why did you get rid of the wagon?"

"Because…" she stated, her eyes filling, "when I looked at the wagon, the memories came flooding back. John… the sweet way he'd say my pet name, Baby Blue."

Kit swallowed, seeing the pain on her grandmother's face. She felt guilty for pressing the point, seeing her grandmother's hands holding her head. "We need to understand."

"You can't if you don't listen to me. Hear my voice. I thought it was sweet of John to name the wagon Baby Blue, after the color of my eyes, you see. It was a reflection of his love for his wife, and for the racing life he loved, too."

"Tell us more, Mother."

"At this age, a woman knows what's important. My family means everything to me. You… mean everything to me."

"We empathize with your caring nature," Michael replied, sighing. "But what does your family have to do with what amounts to giving the wagon away? It was our hope to bring in money to help save the ranch."

She looked directly at her son. "I raised you by myself, without a father. I kept the wagon buried in the barn all these years because John loved it, and it brought me pain just looking at it. So, I hid it away, hoping it would never see the light of day."

"Say it."

"I still see him underneath the wagon, beneath the wheels, even though I was not there. And God help me and give me strength, I never want to see any of you underneath the chuckwagon, too."

Silence. A stillness for the space of several seconds.

"We have a lot to talk about." Michael sighed, searching the expressions of his family. "Maybe my mother, your grandmother, has a point."

"What point?" Cole countered, his voice choked, seemingly not backing down. "If my grandfather were alive, would he want us denying our heritage because of his death? Or would he want us to carry on? I fell off my bike a few times as a kid. Dad, you always said, get back up and ride. How is this any different?"

"John told me more than once…"

"Don't you say it, Bennet Dalton."

"I guess I'll just shut my mouth then, sit down and be quiet, as if I wasn't a part of this family."

Bennet took a seat on the ottoman beside Sam.

"After the work I've done to get this family back in the race," she said, staring, "to save this ranch? The social media marketing?"

"Nothing less than impressive," Jared commented, grinning at Kit's sister.

"Look—" Michael Wheeler appealed for calm. "We're either in this together, or it's finished. Who wants to race?"

All three of the Wheeler grandchildren raised their hands.

"Who's undecided?"

Bennet and Kit's father raised their hands.

"And who is against?"

Gina Wheeler and the matriarch of the family, Dot, raised their hands.

"Mom!" Kit exclaimed in exasperation, "for crying out loud, why are you siding with Gran?"

"Because I'm a mother, too. The reasons don't matter. If your grandmother doesn't want this family in the race, then it doesn't happen. Dorothy Wheeler is the matriarch. Frankly, she should garner more respect from her grandchildren."

Mom usually didn't say much, but when she contributed to the conversation, her words were guaranteed to provoke thought. Kit didn't know how to respond.

"I've had enough of this bullshit," Cole cursed, rising from the sofa. "I'm heading to the tavern."

"Cole! Watch your language," Gina scolded him.

Gabe raised his hands in appeal, looking at Kit for direction. "I could use a drink, too. Do you mind if Kit and I join you, Cole?"

"What about you, Mr. Public Relations?" Sam asked, rising from the ottoman. "Would you buy me a drink at the local Honky Tonk?"

"I'd love to, Miss Wheeler. Do you mind if I drive?"

Sam rose from the couch and stormed off to grab her coat.

"Please do. I'm planning on getting rip-roaring drunk and I won't be able to hold a steering wheel after."

Kit sighed as Gabe breached the gap and reached for her hand. "Come on, darling. Let's go chaperone your family. If no one objects, I'll pay for the drinks."

~

DOT WHEELER's grandchildren sat around a rectangular table at the Honky Tonk Tavern. The boys ordered beer and the girls, cider. Gabe sipped his brew trying to see a positive spin in this family saga, but he wasn't alone in his frustration. Everyone at the table appeared defeated. Glum. He glanced at the tavern walls and the many black and white photographs—chuckwagon images of the Stampede—other success stories that didn't bring comfort to anyone sitting at the table.

Although he was disappointed in Dot Wheeler's decision, he understood her reasoning, too. Only a strong woman would take such a stand and a family had to admire her courage. Though with the wagon gone, there was no means to advertise or promote TarSan Oil. *Darn it!* He had not seen this development coming. He glanced at Jared, studied his expression. Jared was at a loss for words, too.

"So, what now?" Cole asked, taking a sip of amber ale. "Do we accept this outcome, or do we engineer a counterplan?"

"Can't believe I'm sitting at the local tavern," Sam whined, drumming her manicured fingernails on the wooden table. "Sipping a cool one? I should be enjoying a glass of fine wine at an expensive restaurant. Jared was taking me to the Calgary Tower."

Gabe disregarded Sam, his thoughts were on Kit. She held her head in her hands, her eyes downcast. The defeat gutted him. "You okay, darling?"

"I don't know what to say. To you or to Cole. My brother was excited to drive the wagon and now it's over."

"Is this the way it ends?" Sam complained, as sad as her sister. "God, you bought four horses. I was ready to give the race my best effort, being one of the first female outriders."

"This fight has never been about any one of us, the wagon, or even the race. What happens to the ranch if we don't take action? This is my fault. I should have been more sensitive to Gran's feelings. I feel like I've failed everyone."

"You're not a failure. Get your chin up, sis. We're in this together. We've been manipulated, and by our own parents," Cole said with grimace, "the parental units who encouraged us to give our best efforts in everything. To never give in. What a shame."

"I rarely listen to mine," Jared stated with a breathy rasp, raising his hand as if to direct a choir. "Tradition. Values. Morals. What do parents know anyway? We're the Millennials. The generation with a mind to change the world. We can ride out any storm and tackle any problem. Do anything. Visit the moon if we want."

"This is why I hired this guy. Love his go-get-'em attitude," Gabe said with a wink.

Kit's eyes brightened with Jared's enthusiasm, but Gabe could see she wasn't convinced.

"Damn straight," Cole interjected, cheering Jared with his glass. "And we can damn well do anything we want, without getting hurt. We're damn near invincible."

"Do you remember when we were younger?" Kit ruminated, amusement glistening in her eyes. "There wasn't a tree we couldn't climb."

"And Sam only fell that once, and it wasn't far…" Cole added, his eyebrows rising.

"And she didn't break her arm, either." Sam stuck out her tongue at her brother. "Or spend the night in the hospital, never mind an entire summer in a cast."

"Hey, no one made you climb the tree, but getting hurt was not the point I was trying to make. You scrambled up the tree even though you thought you couldn't do it. Sometimes, we have to go where we think we can't."

"It hurt like hell."

"Would you do it again?"

"Probably," Sam said, punching Cole lightly on the arm. "Remember when we took the car…"

"Shut your mouth!" Kit shrieked, shaking her head. "We promised, crossed our hearts and hoped to die, that we'd never talk about 'that little trip' ever again.

"Spill," Gabe remarked. "You can't make a statement like that and not give away the secret."

"You tell him," Sam said, sweet-talking her sister. "It was your idea."

"Nope. I swore myself to secrecy and I mean to keep the peace. Dad still doesn't know."

"I didn't make any pledges," Jared snickered, slamming his drink on the table. "I enjoy a good story as much as the other guy, and I'm good at learning secrets. I'll get to the bottom of this brouhaha."

"Brouhaha?" Sam hooted, breaking into a fit of giggles, "where'd you learn a word like that?"

"Little lady, I'll fricking tell you, if you tell me where you went in the car."

"Sam, you wouldn't dare," Kit appealed, worrying her lip.

Cole stretched forward. "Do I get some say in this? I'm always stuck in the middle of these two sisters, and then an idea amuses them, and before you know it, you're… in a car bound for Edmonton."

"Fuck it." Kit smirked, joining in on the fun. "We were young. What could happen to us now if someone learned the truth?"

"Tell them," Cole pestered, "you're the project manager."

"You're both okay with this?"

Sam raised her hands in supplication as if she didn't know what to do.

Kit gave in. "'Green Day' and 'My Chemical Romance' were playing at the Coliseum. What could we do? We had to see them and unfortunately, they were not playing in Calgary. The best concerts always go…"

"I know, to Edmonton." Gabe took a sip of his beer. "Your dad still doesn't know you borrowed the car?"

"No, he doesn't," Kit lamented. "He thought the three of us were sleeping at friends' houses." She rolled her eyes. "Although he did question how we knew so much about the show."

The Wheeler children stared at each other then, pondering Kit's recollection. *What if Dad had known the truth and had chosen to keep silent?*

"What other trouble did you three get up to?"

"Cole broke Mom's favorite vase."

"Now, that's a crime if I've ever heard one," Gabe snickered, shaking his head.

"It never would have happened if you hadn't insisted on playing flag football in the middle of the living room."

"Samantha hid Mom's wedding ring. She hasn't found it to this day."

Sam's face went white, obviously terror-stricken by the revelation. But when the three siblings burst out laughing, Gabe just about spit his beer on the table. It wasn't funny, but everyone was laughing.

"I was five years old," Sam appealed, tears streaming down her face.

"Sam made a time capsule as part of a school project. The only problem was she took Mom's ring and placed it inside."

"Your mother's ring?" Gabe said with a grin.

"Mom doesn't know to this day what happened. We couldn't bring ourselves to tell her the truth."

"I have a solution. I own a metal detector." Jared raised his hands. "I'd be willing to take up a treasure hunt on your behalf, to locate the missing capsule, if you want."

"I've never thought about searching for it," Sam replied. "Maybe. But we'd have to be careful."

"What about you, Kit? There must be a secret about you?"

Kit's face turned a bright red. "Oh, I don't think so. Nothing comes to mind."

"Kit was an angel." Sam smiled slyly, sipping her cider. "She could never do wrong. Oh, but wait, what about the dormer window?"

"Sam, you wouldn't dare…"

"Gabe, ask Kit about a boy named Aaron."

Gabe glanced at Kit. She was crestfallen. She placed her forehand against her head.

"Whatever it is, it's okay, Kit. You don't have to tell me."

"Oh, she's going to tell you. No one shares my secrets without sharing their own. Fair is fair."

"I can't do it," Kit said, "it's too embarrassing."

"Let me guess, then. Did Aaron climb up the side of the house, sneaking inside your bedroom window?"

Everyone waited. Kit swallowed, then slid her chair back from the table.

"This isn't funny anymore."

"Kit's right," Sam said, "let's forget I said anything."

"Gabe, I've made some mistakes in my life, but permitting a boy to enter the house through my bedroom window, late at night, well, it was a mistake."

Gabe searched her face, seeing how the disclosure upset Kit. But this was her past and he didn't want her thinking this news upset him. "Would you do it again?"

She looked at him, confused. "What do you mean?"

He grabbed her fingers and squeezed. "With me?" he said hopefully.

Kit smiled, glanced at the table and then at him. "You're far too old for climbing lattice and I'm mature enough to lead you inside through the front door."

"What about later tonight? Would you lead me inside?"

She blushed in front of her siblings, leaned closer to him so nobody else could hear. "When can we leave?" she whispered, licking the cider from her lips, "I'm just about finished my drink."

"All right, you two." Cole coughed. "Enough fun and games. When are we talking about Baby Blue? I for one say, parents or no parents, we get the wagon back and enter it in the race, just like we planned."

"All for one and one for all," Sam cried out, "like the good ole days when we were kids."

"You know," Kit said, taking a deep breath, "our conversation has me thinking we've shared good and bad moments. We're richer for our experiences."

"I don't think we're richer." Cole rolled his eyes.

"The point I'm trying to make is life comes with risk, of course it does, but we're not living unless we're climbing the mountain, swimming upstream, or engaging in the race…"

Cole finished his beer and jumped up from his chair. "I'm getting in my truck and going in search of the wagon. Who's with me?"

"Let's do it," Kit yelled. "Let's get our wagon back!"

Just then, the tavern's door opened, and Bennet came inside.

"Damn," Cole interjected, seeing the family friend. "Just when we've got a plan, good ole Bennet stops by."

Gabe could see that Bennet was sadder than a kid who'd lost his candy. He sat at their table and removed his cowboy hat. "Well, don't just sit there looking at me, young 'uns. Get me a beer. It's been a difficult night."

"We're glad you're here," Cole said. "We want you to know we've come to a decision. We're not accepting the situation as it stands. We're getting Baby Blue back. You can either join us or leave us."

"I'll be in a whole heap of trouble if I join you."

The whole table went silent, waiting for someone to speak.

"So, you're in?" Kit hinted, hoping, biting her lip.

"Your grandmother will hurt me, but I'm in!"

"Yay!" everyone cheered.

"Bartender," Gabe called, raising his hand. "Get us another round. We're celebrating."

CHAPTER 15

The Wheeler kids and their guests had consumed way too many drinks, so Bennet, given he was sober, drove the group to the Treasury Branch, but to their chagrin, the wagon wasn't on the property. They spent the next hour driving up and down the village roads searching. They finally sighted the chuckwagon in a locked enclosure near the village council offices. It was risky entertaining the theft. The sheriff vehicles were parked near the lockup, although they were too drunk to care.

It was late at night and dark. The headlights from Bennet's truck lit a chain-link fence. The group crept toward it, trying to exhibit their stealth. Someone laughed.

"Shh…" Kit crooned, trying to keep her voice low while slinking toward the gate, but a cascade of giggles rippled from her throat, too. A finger poked her in the ribs… and she jumped.

"Hey, you. Keep it down, girl."

"Gabe!" she complained, whispering, trying to be quiet. "Don't do that!"

Jared and Samantha drew near. "We don't have to be quiet. Even if someone caught us, what could they do? Technically, the wagon belongs to us."

135

"Tell that to your financial advisor," Bennet replied. "The chuckwagon belongs to the bank now and I'm sure Dot was wise enough to hand them the bill of sale."

Cole, unmindful of the warning, stood near the gate. "It's padlocked." He grabbed the lock and peered at the metal beast, then let it fall against the gate. He didn't seem to care about the clamor, which to Kit, sounded loud.

"I thought of this circumstance," Bennet hedged, "I'll get my bolt cutters."

"Bolt cutters?" Kit heard Gabe say, "why would you have cutters in your truck? Shouldn't you be retired?"

"I like to keep busy and I always come prepared. My father taught me well."

"I don't understand. Why are you helping us, Bennet?"

"I don't rightly know myself. Maybe I want to experience life or maybe I want to run the race again, if you kids will let me."

Bennet walked to the back of his truck, pulled the tailgate down, and then climbed onto the bed. He was soon rifling through his metal tool box. He returned to the gate with cutters clutched in his hands.

"You sure you want to do this, kids? Once we cut the lock, there's no turning back."

"Cut the deadbolt," Cole replied, standing in front of the headlights.

Bennet went straight to work. He grasped the metal shank and bore down, groaning. "Come on, you mother," he ranted, exerting more pressure.

"You want me to help?" Cole asked.

"I have this," he groaned. Suddenly the shank gave way and fell to the ground.

Everyone cheered, clapping.

Whoop, whoop!

Kit gasped, hearing the chirrup of the siren, quickly followed by red and blue flashing lights. They were in trouble.

"Stay where you are," Sheriff Williams declared, leaving his squad vehicle.

"Good evening, Sheriff," Bennet replied.

The sheriff strolled forward studying the group. "What do we have here?" he asked, scrutinizing them. "It's late for a stroll. What are you folks up to? What's that I see in your hand?"

Kit glanced at her brother, Cole. She saw the broken lock. Everyone saw the evidence.

"Nothing." He placed the lock behind his back.

"Look, the gig's up. You're surrounded."

Another set of lights flashed. Kit closed her eyes against the glare and shook her head. How had they missed the patrol cars?

"Look, Sheriff Williams. We're here to collect the wagon. It belongs to our family and we have every right to retrieve it. We're not random thieves."

"Kit Wheeler, I'm surprised at your behavior. This is not like you."

"It's exactly like me to fight for my family and you damn well know what I mean."

"I don't think I do, ma'am." He meandered closer. "Why don't you tell me?"

"Come on, Aaron. I know what this looks like. You've caught us in the act, but we've known each other since we were kids in grade school. Turn around. Look the other way. Let us take what is rightfully ours."

"I want to. I actually placed a bid on the Grande Prairie race. I could use the money, even though," he said snidely, "the whole town knows you'll never win. Still, the law's the law and I've taken an oath to defend it. To serve and protect, people and property. You understand, right?"

Kit took a step toward Aaron. "You're just sore 'cause I never agreed to be your date at the Sadie Hawkins dance."

"Honey," he stated, shaking his head. "That was years ago. I have a wife now and speaking about my lady, it's two in the morning. I'd like to go home. I tell you what, let's call it a night. I can't see myself arresting you. We're old friends for Pete's sake. So, here's what we'll do. You get yourselves inside Bennet's truck, leave peacefully, and I'll pretend I never caught you at the scene of the crime."

"Thank you, Sheriff," Bennet replied. "We'll be on our way, then. Come on, young 'uns. You heard the sheriff. Let's go."

Kit felt angry. "Something stinks here. Of all the nights, why are you parked here, seemingly waiting for us?"

"Your grandmother gave us a call earlier in the evening, warning the law that her grandchildren might be up to some shenanigans. She'll be surprised about you, Bennet."

"Dot put you up to this? That woman. You can't get anything past her."

"Okay, off you go."

Gabe all of a sudden snickered. "Sheriff, are you the boy who climbed through Kit's bedroom window?"

"What window?" His voice took on a more serious tone.

"Small town," Kit said with a grimace. "Gabe, you were bound to meet my former flame. Everyone knows everyone in a small town."

"Okay, enough shenanigans. Go. Home."

Samantha and Jared climbed into the back seat of Bennet's truck. Cole hurried to join them, but not before placing the broken lock in the sheriff's hands.

"I'll be sending you a bill for the lock," Sherriff Williams commented.

"Please do," Kit replied.

"Oh, Kit?" Sheriff Williams hastened to add. "If you want the wagon returned, one of you should make an appointment with your financial advisor. Joel's not happy about owning the wagon."

"If Joel is so concerned about ownership, then why did he purchase it in the first place?" Kit asked.

"It was for sale." He grinned, placing his hands on his hips.

"And better the bank owns the wagon, than some random company who doesn't care about you."

"Frack." Kit kicked at the ground. "We're done. It's over."

"Maybe not."

"What do you know, Aaron?"

"Let me tell you something, little lady. Baby Blue is a positive commodity, but she's meaningless, *worthless*, without her family. Don't tell your grandmother I said this to you."

"You mean we never had to commit a theft?"

"I didn't say anything. Make an appointment with Joel. Good night, everyone."

Sheriff Williams walked back to his car, climbed inside and switched off the flashing lights. He waved and drove away.

"Interesting development," Gabe said, escorting Kit to the truck.

"I guess I have an appointment with our financial advisor in the morning."

CHAPTER 16

"So, you see," Kit explained, studying Joel with a serious expression, "my grandmother should never have sold you our wagon."

Kit was ready to hurt someone. They should have been on the track practicing instead of tracking a chuckwagon. Begging for their own asset. Joel, the family's financial advisor, was the means to having their wagon returned, but he wouldn't cooperate.

"I understand what you think should have happened, but when your grandmother approached me, how could I refuse? Dot Wheeler is a matriarch of your family and to some extent, this community, too. A man doesn't say no to a woman such as she."

It was laughable. He was wrong.

"Joel, you understand the position we're in, right? We're supposed to race Baby Blue in less than four weeks. Not having the wagon in our possession leaves us in a difficult situation."

"I understand. A family without its *perceived property*," he stressed, "is like a tree losing its leaves. Now, our financial institution doesn't like seeing our clients naked, but once the leaves have fallen, it takes some time to see new growth."

"I don't understand what you mean. Let me give you my view

of the circumstances. Property sold to another without the permission of 'all' its stakeholders is likened to a theft. I'm here in good faith to obtain an item that rightfully belongs to me."

"Yes," he said, studying his desk, "and I understand how you might see the matter in such a way. However, as far as the bank is concerned, Baby Blue was sold with the greatest degree of respect. We hold the bill of sale, but I agree with you, it's a sad circumstance."

"Sad? It's downright distasteful. Look, let's get to the point. I need the wagon. Our family can't race without it."

"I agree. I've talked to my superiors and we think we have a solution."

"Well, don't keep me waiting, spit it out."

"Look We accepted the wagon as an asset against your debt load. It seemed like a good deal with the history of the wagon. One might say that the bank could make a good return on the investment, too. There's a problem, though."

"What's that?"

"While the wagon may seem like a valuable commodity, we don't believe the value is as great. The wagon is more of a liability, an expense, unless it's combined with family assets."

"Joel, give this to me in plain language. You're not making sense."

"I've talked to our branch manager at great length. We want you continue with your ambition, to race the wagon. The Treasury Branch is inclined to support the venture, on two conditions."

"Yes?"

"One, the wagon holds a canvas with the Treasury Branch's name. Two, any and all funds earned from the race are returned to us."

"Joel, we were hoping to use any revenue to assist in saving the ranch."

He reached forward and patted her hand. The action surprised Kit. It was unlike this money lender.

"The money would be used to credit your indebtedness," he said, seriously. "Look, the Wheeler family has always been a strong member of our community. Our branch will not be seen as hampering or hindering the family. We're here to offer our financial support and advice if you want it, to get your family back on your feet, however we can. We're not certain the race is the way to do it, but if the family wants to race, then we want to race, too."

Kit's mouth fell open. "I don't know what to say."

"Say you'll put our brand, our name, on your canvas."

Kit brushed a tear from her eye. "How kind of you. To *let* us drive the wagon."

"Perfect," he clapped his hands, clearly excited.

"There's just one thing about the canvas. I'm happy to put the Treasury Branch's name on it, but I have a request."

"I'm listening."

"Somewhere on the canvas, my grandfather's name needs to appear. In memory of John Wheeler."

"We can do that," Joel said with a slight smile.

"When can we pick up Baby Blue? We need to practice."

"What do you propose?"

"Bennet Dalton can arrange for the wagon to be transported to his land. He has a track and he's mentoring us in the race. We won't be confiding in my grandmother until race day. You can understand the reasons why."

"I sure can. Miss Wheeler, you've made me a happy man. I've attended many Stampedes all across the province, but I've never had stakes in the race before. I'll be cheering for the home team. Can't wait for race day."

"Joel, thank you for partnering with us. For the first time in days, there's hope to save our ranch."

"Kit," Joel concurred, emotion rising in his eyes, "there's always been hope."

"I hope we don't disappoint you."

He pushed his chair back from his desk, came around to the front and gave her a firm handshake.

"It's a deal, Kit Wheeler."

"Bennet will be round to collect the wagon. See you at the Grand Prairie Stompede."

"I'll be there."

Kit left the bank in shock. Perhaps the family would be okay after all, but she didn't know what to tell Gabe. They had no choice. They had to place the bank's brand on the chuckwagon's canvas. Where did that leave TarSan Oil and the Bradshaw family?

CHAPTER 17

"*H*ow do professional outriders manage this load?"

Kit had an entirely new respect for the Western sport. She had been practicing with her siblings the entire week, loading and unloading, struggling to climb on a running horse, maneuvering the figure eight, and then exploding down the track. She was exhausted. No matter how fast or how slow the horses ran, they *never* seemed to reach the finish line fast enough. Yet her brother, Cole, drew an impressive smile every single run.

Bennet held a stopwatch in his hands and he counted the seconds of every race. They were never fast enough.

"Let's go again," Bennet said, his eyes wrinkling with concern. "If we have any chance at winning, we have to come close to one minute and seventeen tenths of a second. Kurt Bensmiller's world champion record."

Kit studied Bennet as he strolled toward them. He must have been warm, given that he was dressed in casual Western wear and a navy long-sleeved shirt, but he never lost his cool. Never complained. Was always positive, and encouraged them to try another round, no matter what happened.

"Bennet, we won't better our time as far as I can tell." Sam held her horse near the front of the wagon.

"What was our time?" Cole asked. "Felt fast to me."

"You're gonna cry like a baby if I tell you."

Kit nibbled at her lip, Sam winced. Cocky for a man of seventy-eight.

"Well, we're sure as hell not beating a champion record," Cole said, placing the reins on his lap. "What's the slowest time we have to beat?"

"One minute, sixteen seconds."

"That's quite a gap. What's the average we've achieved so far?"

"One minute eighteen."

"Well—" Cole scratched his head, scrutinizing the track. "How hard can it be to gain two seconds?"

"You can make up time by coming around the barrels smoother, taking to the inner rail faster."

"Easier said than done," Cole complained, wiping his brow, "but I'm sure trying."

"I know you are, son. Now, stop talking about it. Get into position."

Kit groaned but did as Bennet requested. *Why had they fought so hard to be a part of this race?* This was tough work.

At the rear of Baby Blue, Kit sucked in a breath. Her heart was already pounding with anticipation. With her left hand she held her horse's reins, with her right, she held the stove against the ground. She didn't dare let it go. If she lifted the stove before the horn blew, their wagon would gain a full one-second penalty. They knew they'd be slower than other professional drivers, so they couldn't risk any penalties.

"You ready?"

"I'm ready," Sam piped up.

Kit couldn't see her sister, but she didn't sound excited. It was Sam's job to hold the horses and keep the wagon in line with the barrel. All three siblings knew, to win this race, they had to work together.

The horn blew.

Kit threw the stove in the wagon.

"Hah," Cole yelled, slapping the reins. Four thoroughbred horses charged forward, doing a full figure-eight around the barrels. Kit managed to leap on a moving horse, then gave chase, pressing her knees against her mare's side, thundering behind the wagon.

She only had one thought. Run—

She heard the wheels of the chuckwagon grinding against the earth, the harness bells jingling, and the hooves hammering, exploding forward across the track. And Cole...

"Hah," he yelled again, whistling, taking to the inside.

Sam fell in beside Kit. She glanced at her sister briefly, bending low in the saddle and appearing excited. Together, they tore around the track, racing for the finish.

"Easy, girl," Kit said as they crossed the finish line. She patted the mare's neck, permitting her to slow. "Well done, Lacey Lu."

"Yes!" Bennet hollered, expressing his enthusiasm. His smile alone acknowledged their success. He ran toward them. "One minute seventeen. You improved by a full second."

Cole drove the horses forward, a huge smile on his face. "We're catching up enough to come in dead last," he laughed, winking at his sisters. "But seriously, do you think we're ready, Bennet?"

"Well hell, from what I've seen, you've always been ready. Your grandfather would be proud."

"Why the solemn face?" Kit asked, urging her mare closer.

"Miss the man, that's all. If only John had lived to see this day."

Kit, Sam and Cole gazed at each other, all three siblings at a loss for words. Every one of them felt the emotion. Bennet glanced to a place unseen.

"Take the horses to the barn. You know the drill. The horses are watered, brushed, and fed. They've worked hard; they eat first."

"One more week." Bennet placed his stopwatch in his pocket. "You kids ready?"

"Hell, yeah!" Cole roared.

"We got it," Kit acknowledged.

"Kit, have you told Gabe about the canvas? The Longview Treasury Branch canvas arrived this morning."

"No," she said, worrying her lip.

"Don't you think you better?"

"I'll give Gabe a call tonight."

She nudged Lacey Lu in the sides and galloped toward the barn with Sam following close behind. What would she say to Gabe?

THE SUN WAS SETTING by the time Kit left the barn. Sam had left before her and Cole was conferring with Bennet. She'd said her goodbyes and walked to her car. Her cell phone rang. She glanced at the screen and saw Gabe was calling.

"Hi," she said, trying to hide her anxiety, "how are you?"

"I'm fine. I'm not sure I like the sound of your voice. Is everything okay?"

"Yeah, of course. I'm just tired. We've finished practicing for the day, and no day is complete until the horses have been cared for."

"How'd it go?"

"You know," Kit hedged, approaching her vehicle, "not bad. We gained a full second of time."

"That should make you happy."

"Honestly, Gabe," Kit sighed, swallowing, "I've been keeping something from you. I meant to tell you…"

"I'm almost in Longview. Can it wait until I reach the ranch?"

"What?" she laughed nervously. "You're coming my way? I'm surprised. What brings you here?"

"It's been a long week. All hell broke loose at the office, but the bottom line is I've been missing you."

"You miss me?"

"You know I do, honey. Any chance I could stay the night? I looked at the sky and saw the clouds darkening toward the east. Thought there might be a chance of another thunderstorm?"

"Sweetheart, did you pack your pajamas?"

"Will I need them?" He laughed.

"No." She giggled, leaning against her car, excited that her oil man was on his way. "You just keep your hands on the steering wheel and don't speed."

"Hands are on the wheel, honey, but they'd rather be..."

Kit unlocked her car and climbed inside. "I understand. I have to let you go, Gabe. I don't have Bluetooth technology."

"Okay, I hear you. I'll let you go. I'll be at the ranch in about ten minutes."

"I'll be waiting."

Kit pressed the button and ended the call.

"Oh frack," she whispered. There was no getting around the truth. She had to tell Gabe about the canvas and the new company that would support the family.

CHAPTER 18

*K*it and Gabe pulled into the driveway at the same time, but they were not alone in arriving at the ranch. Kit observed Margaret Green, leaning against an old white and blue, beaten-down truck with a trailer attached. Her arms were crossed, and she appeared angry.

"Oh dear," Kit muttered to herself as she exited her vehicle. Gabe gave her a cursory glance, his eyebrows raised in interest. Together, they approached their impromptu guest.

"Hi…" Kit called in greeting.

"Where are my horses?" Marg growled, interrupting Kit's welcome.

"Your horses? Why don't you come inside and we'll…"

"I don't have time for small talk, Miss Wheeler. I've come to check on the welfare of my horses. Did you think I'd sell them to you and not audit your premises? I always ensure my animals go to a good home."

Kit glanced at Gabe in exasperation. He nodded his support.

"They're being well cared for…" Kit remarked, taking a breath, trying to appear calm, but she felt like she might be sick. Not only from this surprising visit, but also from over-exerting herself most of the day.

"Where are they? There's an older mare in the barn and cows in the pasture. Unless my old eyes have deceived me, there are no horses!"

"Oh," Kit said, "I understand why you'd be confused. Please, let me explain."

"You better start before I blow a gasket."

"Margaret, can we talk in the office building instead of the main house? I can make us some coffee. Or we could go into town and have dinner. Gabe and I have not eaten yet."

"We're not going anywhere, not until I've learned the welfare of the horses."

"All right," Kit sighed. "The office is this way. Follow me."

"So, why the secrecy?" Margaret Green asked, tapping her fingers against the table's surface.

"It's a long story," Kit replied, pouring their guest a cup of coffee. "But in short, the horses are at Bennet's ranch. They're well taken care of. In fact, I just returned from his place. Bennet insists on the horses coming first. No different than when they're in your protection, their care comes first. This is why I have not eaten yet."

"I'm glad to hear it." Margaret sighed, calming. "Relaxes me somewhat, but I thought you were keeping them here?"

"That was the plan," Gabe explained, entering into the conversation, "at least until Dot Wheeler sold the chuckwagon."

"You purchased the horses to pull the wagon. Now what?"

"As I said, it's a long story. But in short, the wagon has been returned, but it's at Bennet's place."

"Okay, a better explanation might be due. Why did your grandmother sell the chuckwagon and if it's been found, why isn't it here?"

Kit explained to Margaret Green her family history, especially the part about her grandmother not being over the incident with her grandfather, and her worry over their grandchildren suffering a similar fate. Margaret Green listened carefully and didn't interrupt during the explanation.

"So, you see," Kit breathed, "if we had kept the wagon at the Wheeler ranch, there was concern that Gran might sell it out from under us, again."

"Who bought the wagon?"

"The Longview Treasury Branch."

Kit glanced at Gabe sheepishly, then at the table. His brows furrowed, but he didn't say anything.

"Would you like to see the horses, Margaret? You've come far to audit their care."

"I certainly do." She took a final sip of coffee. "Maybe we could drive together if you don't mind."

GABE OFFERED TO DRIVE, so Kit and Margaret climbed into his vehicle. Kit in front and Margaret Green in the rear passenger seat.

"You're training for the Grande Prairie Stompede," Margaret commented. "How is the training going, and are the horses adjusting to their new roles?"

"They run. They don't complain. How can you tell if they're unhappy? Myself, I never imagined the work would be so hard," Kit replied, scrutinizing Marg. "I have a healthy new respect for the Western sport of chuckwagon racing."

"I've been at work all week. I'm hoping to see Kit and her siblings in action tomorrow. If she'll let me watch," Gabe said.

"Really?" Kit was excited about the news. "You're coming out to watch us?"

"Sure am."

When they pulled into Bennet's place, he must have seen them arriving. He came outside. Approaching the BMW, he accepted Marg's hand in a firm handshake.

"Hello, Marg. Nice to see you. I bet you're here to audit the horses."

"Sure am," she said, laughing and patting Bennet's hand. "How are you, Bennet? Thanks for giving my horses a home. Thought they'd be going to this young lady," she emphasized, "but I hear your girlfriend's been struggling with the Stampede idea. I know something she doesn't."

"What's that?" Bennet laughed, his face turning red.

"A woman can trust you with anything."

"Kind of you to say, too, but this home is temporary. I'm getting too old to manage horses full time. But let me tell you," he said, squinting at Kit and Gabe as if he had a purpose in mind, "I'm trying to inspire the young 'uns to follow in my lead."

"There might be some promise there, too. Can you see the spark in their eyes? It's only matured since the last time I saw them."

"Margaret—" Bennet shook his head, smiling, his cheeks a rosy color. "I wasn't talking about romance."

"I was. A mature woman can sense the mating call a mile away."

"Ha, ha." Gabe laughed, shaking his head. "Maybe we should talk about the purpose for your visit?"

"The horses?" Kit agreed.

"Let's go to the barn, then," Bennet said with a wink, "we're embarrassing them."

The group left the front of the house and walked along a well-worn path until they came to a gate. Bennet opened it, and they followed him. Soon pulling two heavy doors open, they walked inside the barn where the thoroughbreds had been bedded down for the night.

"There's my girls." Margaret strode forward, studying the mares with admiration in her eyes.

Kit watched the older woman, her eyes softening, creasing at the corners. Clearly, she loved her horses and the horses seemed to know it. Lacey Lu came forward, bobbing her head and nickering. Margaret produced an apple from her inside pocket and held it in her hands.

"There you go, my beauty," she cooed, permitting the equine to bite chunks. The apple was soon gone.

She turned to Kit and Gabe, all smiles. "Thank you for giving my girls a good home. Now that I've seen you're taking excellent care of my horses, I need a favor."

Kit leaned against a stall. "What favor?"

Margaret moved onto the next horse and produced a second apple. "I need help at the rescue. I don't have a heart to turn horses away that are in trouble, and I was hoping you'd consider adopting one or two more."

"We adopted eight," Kit said, "but we could use more."

Margaret's expression was deadly serious. "They're not thoroughbreds. They won't help you win a race, but they'll give you a ton of love, and you'll sleep better at night knowing you saved a life."

Kit gazed at the ground. She wanted to help, but who was she kidding, they barely had the funds to care for their current responsibilities. The money earned from the estate sale was quickly depleting. The next mortgage payment was looming.

"I don't…"

"What Kit means to say," Gabe responded, taking her hand, "is this might not be the best time. Let Kit and me talk about it. How many horses need help?"

"I need to find a home for my mare and her colt. Plus, three horses a family couldn't care for any longer, and an abused yearling found at the side of the road. He's so scared, poor little fellow. He needs love and attention. I can't give him that, and…"

Kit nibbled her lip. She saw the emotion pinching Marg's expression. The light that had previously brightened her eyes seemed to diminish. She was obviously seeing the young horse. Her forehead furrowed. Her lips puckered.

"I don't know what to do," she said, staring at them.

Gabe squeezed Kit's fingers.

"Is it too much trouble to bring this little guy here?" Gabe asked Bennet.

"I suppose not. There's lots of space. I don't have many horses anymore, but I can't offer the care part, and Kit, Cole, and Sam, they need to care for the race horses. One horse with behavior problems can be a great deal to cope with. We can't bring him here and not give him proper attention."

Marg gazed at the ground. "Thanks for considering it, at least."

"I'll help," Gabe offered. "Don't worry, Margaret."

"You live in Calgary." Kit replied. "How can you help?"

"Yes," he said, pulling her close. "But I have a feeling I'll be spending much of my time at the ranch. We have a lot to talk about tonight, don't we, honey?"

"We sure do."

AFTER SAYING their goodbyes to Margaret Green, Kit and Gabe withdrew to the office building, a place where they could find some privacy. Near the kitchen space, they sat beside each other on a red tartan couch.

Gabe could smell pizza cooking in the oven, and although the aroma reminded him of his hunger, he remembered the room upstairs, the sanctuary where they had first entertained intimacy. He had plans for this woman and he hoped she'd accept his proposal, but he could tell by Kit's expression that all was not as it seemed, and this was not a moment for romance.

He scrutinized her baby blue eyes, seeing the worry lines marring her forehead. He reached forward and grasped a wayward strand of sandy-blonde hair and swept it away, tucking the lock behind her ear. She leaned into his hand, sighed, then closed her eyes.

"Even a fool could tell something's wrong." He cupped her cheek. "You can tell me."

Kit opened her eyes, pulling away. "I don't know how."

"Is it our relationship? Do you want it to end?"

"No. Nothing's changed between you and me." She stretched forward and grasped his hand. "Confession time. Something has changed, but nothing to do with the way I feel about you."

"Will you make me guess?"

She turned away from him. "It's about the canvas for the wagon."

"It hasn't come? I ordered it two weeks ago. Do you want me to check on it for you? I don't mind, in fact, I'll do it first thing tomorrow morning."

"Gabe," she said, sucking in a breath, "unfortunately, we can't put TarSan Oil's brand on the Wheeler canvas."

Gabe chose to be silent while he contemplated this new information. He scrutinized Kit's face. She couldn't seem to look at him. He watched her fingers, warm against his skin, sliding back and forth across his palm. She made his heart beat faster. He cared for this woman. Cared far more than he ever would about a canvas for a wagon.

He grasped her hand and held it. "There must be a reason why."

"Getting Baby Blue back from the bank came with strings attached."

"Aha," Gabe said, pulling Kit into his arms. "So, the Treasury Branch wants their brand on the wagon and you've agreed to their terms."

"I had no choice. It was the only way our family could race the wagon. But," she continued, searching for the right words, "I've let you down and it feels horrible."

Gabe didn't say anything for the span of several seconds.

"I suppose it's the right step to take, given that they hold the mortgage on the ranch."

"That's what Joel said when I met him at the branch. The partnership seemed the right option to make on behalf of the family, but I want you to know, the decision felt rotten. Still sits like a piece of lead in my gut. I wanted to have the name TarSan Oil on our canvas."

Gabe brought her close to his lips. He kissed her. "It's okay. I have a far better gift than a canvas."

"What's that?"

"I have you. And you know what?"

"What?"

"Let the bank have their canvas. I aim to put the company brand in a far better place."

"Where's that?"

"Your finger!" He laughed, squeezing her hand, massaging her ring finger.

She pulled away, engaging his expression with incredulous eyes. No sign of worry but certainly surprise. "Gabe Bradshaw, what exactly are you saying?"

"I'm going to marry you. That's what I'm saying."

"You've only known me for a month."

"A man can tell."

She held out her hand, palm facing up. "Put your money where your mouth is, sweetheart."

He reached inside his pocket and pulled out a white velvet ring box. He laughed when her eyes widened in surprise.

"What's that, Gabe?"

He put the box in her hand. "Flip the lid, find out."

She opened the box and stared at the ring for several seconds. He waited patiently, watching the emotion overcome her. Her hand went to her mouth, her eyes filled with unshed tears. "Gabe?"

He dropped to one knee. He took the sapphire from the box. "Kit Wheeler, will you marry me?"

"I can't believe this is happening."

"I'll love you forever."

"No man has ever knelt before me."

"I'll keep you in sickness and in health."

She kissed his lips. "I've never even asked you how you feel about children."

"Children? Best we talk about grandchildren. They're the ticket to my mother's heart. You'll have to give her some."

"I hardly know you."

"Kit, a question is on the table. It's waiting to be answered."

She joined him on the floor. She grasped his hand. "Do you mean this? Are you proposing to me?"

"I am."

"I'll marry you, Gabe Bradshaw. I'll love you for the rest of my life!"

He smiled. "The pizza might be burning."

Kit burst out laughing. Shaking her head, she jumped up from the floor and raced to the oven. "Who cares about food in a moment like this." She grabbed the oven gloves, opened the door and saved the pizza. "I've lost my appetite."

"Not me," Gabe replied. "I'll thank you to slice the pizza and bring it over here."

She did as he asked. "You'll be disappointed. There might be burn spots on top."

He took his plate. "Just the way I like it!"

CHAPTER 19

*R*ace day at the Grande Prairie Stompede arrived. Friends, family, and fans, even her future in-laws, were seated in the stands to support the Wheeler kids. Everyone, with the exception of her parents and grandmother, who still didn't know their legacy was soon to race. How she'd kept the secret from her parents with the media attention, Kit didn't know.

The raucous noise from the stands carried to her make-shift barn and the close proximity of other drivers made Kit nervous. She wasn't so sure anymore that she belonged in this race, and one or two curious stares from hopeful contenders seemed to imply to her that their family should save their embarrassment, give up, and walk away.

But their mindset had changed. The Half Mile of Baby Blue wasn't only about the ranch. Not even the three grandchildren who wanted to win the purse. The Stampede owed an inheritance to John Wheeler's memory and Kit Wheeler aimed to run the half mile of Hell, if only to collect the sacrament at the end.

She reflected on the rules of the race that Bennet had taught them while preparing the horses. Sam was taping Ginger and Big Red and Cole tackled the same measures for Tanner and Mischief.

158

Kit had preferred to keep to herself and had finished caring for Old Faithful and Lacey Lu. She ran her fingers over the withers, and Lacey Lu shivered.

"It's okay, girl," Kit said, patting her neck. "I'm as nervous as you must feel, and I'm not the one who has to run."

"You're talking to a horse, you know."

Kit turned, sighting Gabe. She smiled slightly. "You think Lacey Lu doesn't understand where she is or what she's about to do?"

"I see the blue tape on her legs. She probably has an idea what's up, but if you ask me, it's my girl who looks nervous."

"Is it obvious?" she asked, taking a deep inhalation of air.

He came forward and pulled her into his embrace. "I wish I could help you."

"It's a lot of work preparing for the race. Before tomorrow's heat, maybe you could help us tape? Maybe give the horses a bath later tonight?"

"I'd love to." Gabe kissed her forehead. He released her and made to walk away, but then turned to face her.

"You know, Kit, this is probably not the best time to discuss a branding idea with you, but I've had a discussion with my team at TarSan Oil that I'd like to talk to you about. Might help calm your nerves?"

"Oh, yeah?" Kit said, grabbing a brush. "Tell me about it."

"Margaret Green's request of taking on more horses made an impression on me. What do you think about starting a horse rescue center of our own?"

Kit stopped brushing Lacey Lu. She turned to Gabe. "Are you serious? It's a lot of work caring for horses."

"We'd hire help. My dad likes the idea. It's something more substantial than putting a canvas on a chuckwagon, and it could support the industry. You know, we could not only support rehoming equines, but could go further, researching equine care, veterinarian treatments, and even behavioral techniques."

Kit stepped toward Gabe. "You've thought about this."

"My father and I, well… We don't want to force you to come work for us, though we know you're currently without a job, but, maybe you could manage the society?"

"I just said I'd be your wife, you want to employ me now, too?"

"I want to build a life with you. I'm surprised to learn that I want to help animals, considering their welfare."

"What will we call the rescue?"

"Tiffany wants us to name it after her, and she wants…"

"I know," Kit giggled, brushing Lacey Lu, "she wants the yearling who's in trouble."

"Yes, she does."

"I have a wedding gift for you, too!"

"We haven't even set the date yet."

"Do you want to?"

"I was thinking of a long engagement. Maybe next summer?"

"Totally doable, but I'd like to give you my gift sooner."

"You can tell me, Gabe. I'm listening."

"Margaret Green has sent Jewel and her foal, Pepper, to Bennet's ranch as a wedding gift. He's agreed to keep them there until I can purchase us some land. A place to invest in our future. Our own ranch."

Kit shook her head, but she grinned. How was this happening to her?

"You've got this all planned, don't you?"

"I sure do, honey, but it's almost race time. I best take my place near the stands. Now, you take care of yourself. Be careful. Be safe. I'll be watching near the track."

She stepped forward and kissed him. She wouldn't admit how frightened she was.

CHAPTER 20

The horn blew—

Sam released the team of horses and Kit threw the stove into the back of the wagon.

"Hah," Cole yelled, slapping the reins against the horses' backs. They charged forward, their hooves hoeing the track, kicking up dirt.

"And they're off," the announcer called, "charging around the barrel…"

Holding tight to her horse, Kit ran across the mud-laden ground, soon leaping onto Lacey Lu's back. She gave her horse her head, holding on tight with her knees and thighs, urging her around the barrel, and following the wagon as it made its counter-clockwise figure eight.

"Yah," Cole screamed, coming out of the turn, harboring two opponents' wagons on either side.

What happened next seemed to occur in slow motion. The wagons punched forward, everyone aiming for the rail. Cole maneuvered to the inside. Kit watched in horror, seeing there wasn't enough room, but her brother was determined. The quickest time would come in running the inside rail. He urged the horses toward the barrier and the wagon banked left, rising off the ground, its wheels spinning in the air.

Cole flew.

Kit screamed.

Horrified, she watched her brother sail through the air and land on the ground, to lie on the dirt like a lifeless rag doll. The wagon righted itself and the wheels bounced on the track. The horses, no longer manned by a driver's hands, rushed onward, racing, exploding along the track.

Help her brother, or stop the wagon?

Sam gazed at her and they both knew what they had to do.

Kit said a prayer that help would arrive for Cole, then pressed forward, kneeing Lacey Lu in the side. "Hah, girl," she screamed, no longer thinking about a win, racing to catch up to the Wheeler's rig, one sister charging to the right-hand side, and Sam pulling for the left. Seconds passed as they came around the track trying to catch up to their wagon.

Kit heard her own heart beating—pounding—threatening to burst free from her chest, and her breath, whooshing, in and out…
Closer, just a little closer…

Nearing the rear end of the wagon, Kit ignored the other teams who were just ahead. She knew her brother lay on the ground and four chuckwagons—one driverless—charged around the track. Teams came around the bend, already halfway around, closing the gap to the finish line.

Her brother was on the ground, in danger of being trampled…

"Hah, Lacey Lu," she begged, urging her mare forward. "Run…"

She passed Baby Blue, catching the tail-end of the team. She could see the lead reins dangling, slapping up and down, trailing on the ground. If she could reach…

Three-quarters around the track, they were coming around the final bend. Sam reached for the lead horse first and took hold of the harness. Kit followed suit. They guided the team to the outside track, knowing the best they could hope for was to slow four powerful horses down.

The lead wagon crossed the finish line, then merged to the outside as well.

The worst feeling was knowing two sisters had to take care of their horses while their brother lay on the ground.

A group of people already surrounded Cole. Kit held her breath as the team passed by. She couldn't tell his condition, or how badly he was hurt. Sam and herself were soon joined by other outriders, and with their help were able to slow the horses to a trot, and then, stop them altogether.

Kit jumped to the ground, prepared to run toward her brother. An outrider grabbed her arm and held her.

"You best stay here, Miss Wheeler."

"My brother," she explained, her voice choking, "he's hurt. I have to…"

"I understand, ma'am," he said, his voice soothing, his eyes dead serious. "I've seen wrecks before. Help's coming."

Help? She felt helpless. She remembered her grandmother's warning, her grandfather's death. History had repeated itself, but in cunning disguise. Guilt lay heavy at her feet, broken on the ground and her gut twisted, needling her ribs harder than the horses that had run the track. She was going to be sick. What would she tell her father? Her mother?

She was the project manager of this ambition. Kit Wheeler was responsible for the welfare of her siblings. She didn't know what to say when Sam grasped her hand and squeezed her fingers, but as two sisters gazed at each other, they knew…

The Half Mile of Baby Blue was a failure.

LATER, Kit sat at Cole's bedside. Tears streamed down her face.

"Hey now," Cole placated, "don't cry, big sis. It's going to be okay."

She sniffled. "I can still see you lying on the ground."

"Hurt like hell, taking that fall. Saw a few stars, I don't mind telling you. With those two wagons on either side, I thought I was a goner."

"Well, it's over, we're pulling Baby Blue from the race."

"Like hell you are," Cole stated, "nothing's changed. We still have a race to run."

"Cole, it's time to admit defeat. Our grandfather was a trained racer. We're playing a dangerous game. Who will fall from the wagon next?"

"God damn it, Kit, if I have to get my ass out of this bed and crawl back to the track, our wagon is racing."

"You and what driver?" Sam asked, unconvinced. "You've got a broken arm. No way I'm driving that rig."

"It will have to be you, Kit."

"No way," Gabe stated, deadly serious. "My future wife is not climbing on that wagon. I won't see her lying on the ground. Seeing you just about killed me."

"You're engaged?"

"Yes." Kit smiled, glancing at Gabe.

"Perfect," Cole commented. "This is what we'll do. Kit drives the wagon. Sam leads the team. Gabe Bradshaw throws his brand, I mean the stove, in the wagon."

"What?" Gabe rolled with laughter. "That's a comedy of errors waiting to happen. I'm a businessman, not an outrider."

Just then Michael and Gina Wheeler hurried inside the hospital room, with a sheepish Bennet following closely behind.

"Cole," Gina Wheeler cried out, rushing to her son's bedside. "My poor boy. I heard you fell. Is the news true?"

"It's true." Kit sighed, feeling guiltier than ever now that her parents were here to view her shame. "The Wheeler family participated in the Stompede." She cried at the sight of her mom. "I'm sorry, Mom. You were right. We were wrong."

Michael shook his head. "Whose idea was this?"

All three of the Wheeler siblings studied each other. "Mine!" Kit, Sam, and Cole replied at the same time.

"Figures," their father grunted, shaking his head. "You kids. You entertain these foolish acts and think we don't know. Think we're none the wiser."

"There's four days left in the Stompede." Cole sat up taller in the bed, wincing when he tried to use his arm. "Kit has to drive."

"Cole… you have to stop this nonsense," Kit pleaded. "A woman cannot drive a chuckwagon. I'm not strong enough."

"I don't know about that," Gabe said with a grin. "You could do anything you put your mind to."

"I didn't think you wanted your soon-to-be wife driving a wagon?"

"What? Has there been talk of marriage?" Michael Wheeler grinned.

"I'm marrying your daughter, Mr. Wheeler, if you'll grant me permission to take her hand."

"I don't need authorization," Kit replied. "I'm an adult, not a child."

"Can we revisit the conversation at hand?" Cole pleaded, appearing angry. "Kit. Please…"

Kit searched her brother's eyes, seeing his pain. The bruises on his face. Sure, he had a broken arm; he was lucky he wasn't nursing a broken neck. "Cole. Please…"

"Bennet, you need to talk to my siblings. Talk some sense into them."

"I'm in a bit of trouble here, son. I'll support whatever decision is made but I can't help with the end result. You kids began this journey, now you have to finish it, too."

"He's right," Sam said, gazing at her brother.

"I'll give you one piece of advice," Bennet asserted, his tone serious. He studied their parents and then the younger generation. "Don't let fear form a part of the decision-making."

"Bennet Dalton!" Gina Wheeler huffed, pointing, "do you see my son in that bed?"

"Sure do, ma'am," he replied. "Brave man lying there."

"Damn straight," Cole grinned. "I'll have you know until I kissed the ground, I was having the best day of my life. Felt great."

"How does it feel now?" Kit asked, unable to look away from the bruises, or the cast.

"Kit, quit looking at me like that. Get past the obvious. You're pissing me off."

"Gabe, what should I do?"

Kit watched the emotions cross her fiancé's face. He didn't say anything for the span of several seconds, and then he took her hand. "I'll support whatever decision this family makes. You run; I'll run right beside you."

"Holy half mile of Hell," Kit sighed, her face flaming with heat. She glanced at her brother and saw his lips lift into a subtle grin. The room went silent. She glanced at her father. Her mother. Bennet.

"I won't help you with this, and it's killing me not offering my opinion, but if you decide to take this risk, I'll be there at the side-lines," Michael Wheeler said. "I'll support whatever decision you make."

"Bennet, do you think I can drive Baby Blue?"

"Do you have hands to hold the reins?"

"Yes," Kit replied, not feeling happy about the sudden pressure, "but they're not as strong as a man's."

"I can offer advice, but you know how to drive the rig. There's a reason why I had you exercise the team a time or two."

She took a deep breath. "Bennet, we'll need your help putting this new team through its paces. Gabe has experience riding a horse, but I'm certain he's never ridden a thoroughbred."

"What are you talking about. All horses run. A nudge in the flanks and away we go, honey."

"Gabe Bradshaw, this is not a time for humor."

"It's exactly the time. You set on driving?"

"I guess, I am. It appears you'll brand the race with your presence after all."

CHAPTER 21

*K*it was exhausted the next morning. Bennet had put Gabe, Sam and herself through their paces running the circuit the previous evening and they had managed marginally well as a team, but was the effort worth the risk? She knew they wouldn't win the race. It wasn't fair to their horses, and driving against teams who had years of experience? Hell, other drivers had family legacies of racing the half mile. Her team might as well load their horses and head on down the road.

And now Melissa Faraday of Global News wanted to interview her, and she'd reluctantly agreed. Gabe led the gorgeous woman into the makeshift stable, with a cameraman trailing behind.

"Kit Wheeler," the reporter called out, smiling as she came forward, extending her hand in greeting. "It's a pleasure to meet you. Thank you for agreeing to this interview. How's your brother faring today?"

Kit poured a mixture of oats and other nutrients into a bucket, then placed the bucket on a hook near Lacey Lu's head. The mare immediately began eating. Kit smiled despite her apprehension. "As hungry as ever. Can't keep a good man down for long."

"Do you mind if we roll the camera?"

"Might as well," Kit replied. "You're welcome to come over here by the trailer. We can sit."

"Oh, that's okay," she replied, coming closer, holding a microphone in her hand. "Our viewers will enjoy seeing you standing beside the horses."

"If not the wagon," Kit replied, winking, "but I need to keep working. So much to get ready, you understand."

"Of course. Are you ready?"

"Yes. I think so."

Kit glanced at Gabe. He was dressed in a beige shirt, blue jeans and brown cowboy boots, and the clothing seemed out of place. But when he smiled, she was put at ease, and more prepared to take on this interview.

"Cam, roll the camera please."

Kit didn't have long to wait before the first question came her way. "Miss Wheeler, I was standing on the sidelines yesterday when your rig lost control. I'm sure I don't have to tell you how devastating it was to watch, but in light of the accident, why are you resuming the race?"

"I was in the race yesterday, Miss Faraday."

"Yes, but you're driving the wagon, isn't that true?"

Kit grabbed a brush and curry comb and began brushing Lacey Lu. "It's true."

"Why, if you don't mind me asking?"

Kit glanced at the reporter, giving serious thought to the question. "We talked about the race as a family and it's pretty simple. We want to continue."

"You'll be the second female driver to race at the Grande Prairie Stompede. How do you feel about that?"

"Don't make too much of it. I don't want my gender to overshadow the reason for being in this race in the first place."

"Remind our viewers, what is your rationale for continuing?"

"It's simple. No different than the other drivers chasing the half mile, we want to win."

"But the odds, they're stacked against you?"

"She knows what she's facing," Gabe piped up, coming to stand beside her.

"Mr. Bradshaw, it's an interesting development seeing the president of TarSan Oil assuming a position as an outrider. Do you care to comment?"

"I'd do anything for my fiancée."

Kit smiled, shook her head, giggled. "He didn't get his way with having the canvas on the wagon, so thought he'd put a band of gold on my finger."

"So, a family race has become a love story, is that right?"

"You got it," Gabe replied, taking her hand, "and we're in this together."

"Is there anything else you'd like to say?"

"Yes," Gabe hastened to add, "TarSan Oil has invested in the Wheeler family by purchasing the horses for the race. I want your viewers to know that I've been so taken with the issues facing equines that my father and I have decided to purchase land and build an equine rescue center."

"That's quite the announcement," Melissa Faraday said in response. "How do you feel about this new development, Kit Wheeler?"

"I'm excited about it, actually. I'll put my project manager skills to work for the sake of equine care."

"Will we see you on the race track after the Stompede?"

"Honestly," Kit breathed out, thinking about it. "I wish it was Cole holding the reins. I'm driving this week to pay tribute to our grandfather, John Wheeler, and hopefully, we win the half mile of Hell in his memory."

"Well, best wishes, Kit. And good luck." One look at the cameraman and he lowered his camera.

"Thank you for this interview. I know it will mean a lot to our viewers."

"You're welcome."

Melissa reached forward and shook her hand. "I wish you well and can't wait to watch the race. A girl can win, you know."

"Thank you." Kit smiled, gazing at her feet. "I appreciate your support."

"No more accidents," Melissa Faraday stated, then stepped away.

"Don't worry," Gabe replied, completely serious. "I'll catch her if she falls."

CHAPTER 22

*T*he sun dipped behind cumulus clouds. Puffy white and spotted gray in places, they stretched as far as the eye could see. The wind had risen, and Kit could smell the rain in the air, but she hoped the precipitation would hold off until after the race. It was nearing the hour when she'd drive the team from the make shift barn to the track. She assessed the horses and their gear, checking the harnesses, the buckles and the lines. The fastenings seemed in proper working order.

"Kit?" She turned to the familiar voice.

"Gran…" she cried out, surprised to see her grandmother, and Gabe too, standing nearby. "What are you doing here? I didn't think you'd come."

"Well," she said, clearly considering, "I'm not rightly sure why I'm here. All I can say is that this possum you're marrying might have had something to do with it."

"Really, Gabe?"

"I thought your lovely grandmother might want to wish her granddaughter well on race day."

"Gabe. That's kind of you."

Kit perused her grandmother's expression. Her baby blue eyes were bright, and watery. She ran her wrinkled fingers through short and curly gray hair. It didn't escape Kit's notice that her Gran wore Western gear. A baby blue shirt that mirrored the color of her eyes, belted jeans and tan leather boots. Kit waited patiently, pondering, what she might say.

"Are you determined to take this on?"

"Determined?" Kit sighed, taking a step forward. "To be honest, Gran, I'm not sure of anything."

"You don't have to drive. We can work out the financial woes without taking a risk on the race. Gabe has assured me of that."

Kit glanced at her soon-to-be husband. *Yes*, he nodded but he didn't say a word.

"Gabe Bradshaw, what have you been telling my grandmother?"

"We had some time to discuss business affairs during the ride from the ranch. No different than the bank placing a canvas on the wagon, there's ways I can support the ranch and make it profitable again. I'd like to help in more tangible ways to achieve a win, better ways than racing. I'm soon to be a part of this family and I don't want my wife driving a chuckwagon. At least not long term."

"What's your point?"

Her grandmother raised her hand. "Chuckwagon racing is part of our past, you know that, Kit. It's not our passion. Look at the other drivers'? You can tell. The fire lives in their veins. They love this Western sport."

"Did my grandfather love this sport?"

"He did. No sense in denying it."

"I could love this sport, too, if given a chance. I see what you two are up to, trying to get me to throw in the towel and give up. I won't do it. It's too close to race time. We'd be laughingstocks. Besides, I promised Cole."

"I don't care what anyone thinks," Gran replied, striding closer and grasping her arm. "My grandson was hurt yesterday. Gratefully, bones mend and bruises heal. In time. Please, Kit…"

Kit gulped, seeing tears filling her grandmother's eyes.

"Don't take the team onto the track."

Kit turned away from her grandmother. She leaned against Big Red and closed her eyes. The horse nickered.

"Oh, Gran, please don't make me emotional."

"I love you, Katherine. I appreciate all you've done to try and save my ranch. My home for over fifty years. You've done it. You've given my life-blood back to me. You don't have to take these horses onto the track. We've already won."

Kit wiped a tear from her eye. She refocused her attention, facing Gabe and her grandmother. "I don't know what to do. I promised Cole."

"He'll understand." Gabe stepped closer, pulling her into his arms.

Suddenly Sam approached. Dressed. Ready. She hid her thoughts better than anyone. Didn't even ask why Gran was at the Stompede. "Family meeting?"

"I might as well tell you, Gran and Gabe think we shouldn't race."

"I didn't say that," Gran countered, glancing at Sam. "I just wanted you to know you don't have to."

Kit stood there, thinking. She studied the team of horses, ready to go. She glanced at her family, trying to make the right decision. "What would grandfather do in this situation?"

Gran laughed, her eyes lit up. "He'd race like a mad devil. Push to the inside and wouldn't give in. Not for anything. I thought it was great, until…"

Kit pondered her grandmother's words as the image registered in her mind.

"I've made my decision, Gabe. Gran. One last time, we're racing the half mile of Hell, in honor of John Wheeler. But after this race, you have my solemn promise. I'll never run the track again. Of course, I can't make the same assurances for Cole. He seems taken with the sport, despite his injuries."

"You sure you want to do this?" Gabe asked.

"Yes."

"Okay." Gran seemed to accept the decision. She approached the team, the horses, and began a methodical check. Kit watched her assess the buckles, her fingers sliding along the lines, maybe ensuring they were strong and properly fastened. She then scrutinized each horse.

"I always loved the horses," she admitted, clearly admiring. "This one, this gorgeous gray…"

"Lacey Lu?" Kit affirmed.

"Put her in front."

"Does this mean I'm riding?" Gabe asked.

"Mr. Bradshaw, are you intent on marrying my granddaughter?"

"I am, ma'am."

"Then saddle up for the ride, Gabe Bradshaw. See this race through to the end and take care of my granddaughter. The team's about to depart."

KIT FELT the wagon moving beneath her while waiting for the horn to blow and the race to start. Shifting, swaying, as if the four-in-hand team were eager to get underway. She'd followed her grandmother's advice and had reassigned Lacey Lu to the front of the team. Lacey Lu was now the lead horse on the left-hand side of the rig. She grunted, neighed, and pawed the ground. Kit couldn't read the mind of a horse, but this thoroughbred rescue seemed eager to run. Margaret Green would be proud.

Kit held the reins in her hands, the leather looping over her thumbs. She glanced at Sam in the front, holding the horses to the right side of barrel number one. She winked at her sister, clearly ready and proud to enter this race with her.

She glanced at the rear of the wagon where Gabe held the stove. She could barely see him with the Treasury Branch's canvas surrounding the top ring. She'd given him his final instructions: *Hold your horse's reins; hold the stove against the ground. Don't release either until we're underway.* She smiled. He winked. They made a good team.

He'd given her some choice words, too. *Please. Don't. Fall.*

Now it was up to skill, the horses, and perhaps a little luck, too.

For you, Cole, and you too, John Wheeler...

The horn blew—

"There's the horn," the announcer drawled, "and the charge is underway..."

"Hah," Kit yelled, slapping the lines on the horses' backs, taking them to a trot and maneuvering them around the barrels, executing the figure-eight as best she could. When Kit drove the team around the second barrel, she had a strange feeling in her gut, as if someone sat beside her on the wagon seat, guiding her. But that was crazy. She quickly dashed the thought away.

"Yah," she yelled again, sighting a wagon to her right and encouraging the team to a gallop. She was in good position to slide to the inner rail and she fought hard to get there.

"Come on, Lacey Lu," she screamed, racing along the dirt track. "You too, Big Red."

The team on the right was soon neck and neck with her team.

"Hah," she yelled, pulling the cross lines, pleading with her horses to run faster.

She thought she heard fans chanting her family's name, but she couldn't be sure of anything other than the clamor of noise, the sound of the wagon bouncing, horses' hooves thundering, exploding along the half-mile of Hell. The din concentrated her hearing.

"Yah," she screamed, halfway around the track.

You've got this...

"Hah," she yelled, as the wagon beside her took the lead, her opponent tried to maneuver to the inner rail. She couldn't let him pass. And her horses seemed to have a will of their own, as if this legendary race was as much a battle for the equines as it was for their driver. They increased their pace, charging around the final bend. Still, the other team was ahead…

"Hah," Kit screamed. The adrenaline pumped through her veins. Her breath puffed from her mouth. She fought hard to the end, soon crossing the finish line.

She glanced at her opponent, permitting her horses to slow at their own pace. She couldn't help but smile, gliding along the track that other drivers had passed across. Every one of them hoping for a win. A huge smile lit her expression. The opposite driver grinned at her and offered a thumbs-up. She accepted his greeting, laughing aloud, hoping his greeting was positive, in that a family belonged here.

She hadn't won the race, but she felt like she'd put on a good show.

And then she did hear her name being chanted from the stands. She glanced at the crowd and waved, not believing she'd just raced: *The Half Mile of Baby Blue.*

CHAPTER 23

*K*it had risen early in anticipation of the Calgary Stampede Parade. The entire Wheeler family was excited to participate, not only in the parade, but also at the Grandstand Show. Cole might feel defeated to not be able to race Baby Blue, but everyone else was over the moon to have the wagon on the Stampede track, no matter how it got there.

It had been a test of wills to decide who would drive Baby Blue along the parade route, and in the end, Gran had decided it should be Kit. After all, she had broken Cole's training record by coming in second at the Grande Prairie Stompede, achieving a time of one minute fourteen seconds. Not bad for a girl.

But Gran told everyone who would listen the team had earned second place and not dead last because of a rescue horse named Lacey Lu. Dot Wheeler had proudly proclaimed that a grandmother had wisdom to share after all, having suggested the mare be placed out front in the first place.

Kit held the reins and led the team along the parade route, pausing from time to time to wave at admiring fans. It was a disappointment to some that the Wheeler family wouldn't race at the Calgary Rangeland Derby, but in fairness to other drivers, the

178

Wheelers were rookies and didn't qualify against professional drivers. Not with race experience, or time.

Kit had been surprised when a representative from the Greatest Outdoor Show on Earth had approached her, asking if she'd consider being a part of the Grandstand Show. This year's theme was a nod to chuckwagon history and a time when cooks would race to the next big stop on the trail. A time when cowboys lived a life on the open prairie, serving up food from the back of their wagons. She had accepted the invite, thinking it was a good way to honor her family and their own Western heritage.

And given that she'd be compensated for her time, the funds were a help to continue paying the ranch's bills, even if Gabe was determined to find oil on their land. Texas tea? She shook her head. His team would never find it.

A horse trotted next to her and a handsome cowboy dipped his hat. None other than her husband-to-be, Gabe Bradshaw. Kit blushed, smiling. She had asked him to sit beside her, since they were getting married, but he'd refused, stating that he was her outrider, and an outrider was nothing without his horse.

Grandmother Wheeler sat beside her instead, with her own cowboy following close behind the wagon, Bennet Dalton. Perhaps remembering a time when he had been an outrider, too.

It seemed fitting. Probably the first time her grandmother had sat on the bench seat in fifty years and she seemed to be enjoying it. A huge smile crossed her face. Kit wondered what her Gran might be thinking. It was good to be on the same side and see her happiness.

A few people sat in the back of the wagon, too. The entire Bradshaw family rested on bales of hay, waving to the passing crowd. No one happier than little Tiffany, who had a hard time staying put. Michael and Gina Wheeler were there, and Cole, still in his cast. Everyone waving. Everyone smiling. Great fun being a part of a parade.

Kit felt super. It proved a point to her. Anything was possible.

Families could overcome any obstacle as long as they were willing to listen to each other, play together, and work hard. If anything, this was what racing *The Half Mile of Baby Blue* had taught her. Sometimes, a family had a distance to go to achieve success.

It didn't escape her notice either that one Jared Wang had joined them this morning. He kept glancing at Samantha. They still had a date to go on, after all.

Kit waved to her sister, riding behind the wagon. Sam smiled, waving in return.

The horses kept trotting, easily making their way forward.

"Hah," Kit called out, urging the team onward and maintaining an easy trot. She knew the best was yet to come. Cole planned to race again next year. Who knew what could happen. Maybe next year, they'd win!

Love the novel you just read?
Your opinion matters.

Review this book on your favorite book site, review site, blog, or your own social media properties, and share your opinion with other readers.

Thank you for taking the time to write a review for me!

AFTERWORD

Every story begins with a premise of an idea. One morning over coffee and a writing date, three authors contemplated writing a series of books loosely related to the Calgary Stampede. When I had my colleagues convinced, Katie O'Connor and Win Day, the Women of Stampede was soon a race in itself. To find authors who shared our vision, and then to contemplate what our stories might be about. My only sadness at the conclusion is that Win Day, the author of *On a Whim* and *Treasure in the Library*, was unable to complete her book. I hope someday, she'll write her story.

I always search for the gold nugget in my stories. In this one, I contemplated whether a woman has ever run the half mile of Hell at the Calgary Stampede, and if not, why not? How could I make it happen for my heroine in my book?

I felt it was important to give Kit Wheeler the opportunity to race. One Beta reader felt it was unlikely. Given my mom could drive a Cat Tractor as a young adult, I don't believe that's true at all. Rilee Letendre will make her debut at the Grand Prairie Stompede this year. So exciting. Go Rilee, go!

I wanted Kit to win! But she came in second place at the Grande Prairie Stompede as I didn't think first place was plausible against professional chuckwagon drivers. I tip my pen to them for their courage. From watching videos of the sport, I can see that chuckwagon drivers, outriders, helpers and families love their Western sport as much as I love storytelling.

My story is fictional, but if a family were serious about racing, they would require a wagon that complies with today's standards, and more training would be required than the glimpse provided in my book. A rescue horse probably wouldn't be able to race, but it's nice to think that horses whose futures are uncertain might have a half-mile more to run.

Of interest to some readers: I learned in my travels to Australia that there was a race horse that no one believed in. A horse who surprised and earned a win! So... don't ever count a family out of the race, or even a horse! No one should ever give up on their life ambitions. One just needs 'the will' to try.

I loved writing this book. I hope you've enjoyed reading: *The Half Mile of Baby Blue.*

WOMEN OF STAMPEDE SERIES

Saddle up for the ride! The Women of Stampede will lasso your hearts! If you love romance novels with a western flair, look no further than the Women of Stampede Series. Authors from Calgary, Red Deer, Edmonton and other parts of the province have teamed up to create seven contemporary romance novels loosely themed around The Greatest Outdoor Show on Earth… the Calgary Stampede. Among our heroes and heroines, you'll fall in love with innkeepers, country singers, rodeo stars, barrel racers, chuckwagon drivers, trick riders, Russian Cossack riders, western-wear designers and bareback riders. And we can't forget our oil executives, corporate planners, mechanics, nursing students and executive chefs. We have broken hearts, broken bodies, and broken spirits to mend, along with downed fences and shattered relationships. Big city lights. Small town nights. And a fabulous blend of city dwellers and country folk for your reading pleasure. Best of all, hearts are swelling with love, looking for Mr. or Miss Right and a happily ever after ending. Seven fabulous books from seven fabulous authors featuring a loosely connected theme—The Calgary Stampede.

WOMEN OF STAMPEDE BOOKS

CONTACT SHELLEY KASSIAN

Dear Reader,

If you're interested in receiving advance news on such items as:

- Book Signings and Event Dates
- Special Pricing Promotions
- Announcements of New Releases
- Advance Giveaways of my Books
- Insights into my Creative Process
- Insights into my Characters and their Stories

Sign up for my newsletter: http://eepurl.com/drzML9

I enjoy hearing from my readers. Have something to say?
Send me a message at: shelleykassian@gmail.com.

ABOUT SHELLEY KASSIAN

SHELLEY KASSIAN, a multi-published author, appreciates the corridors of medieval history and in particular the Tudor period. She has visited the United Kingdom, touring many castles in her pursuit of story. When asked, Shelley assists novice writers in building fictional worlds and enjoys crafting her own stories into novel-length fiction. Shelley shares her life with her husband, adores her adult children, and lives in Calgary, Alberta, Canada.

Visit her website at https://shelleykassian.com
Follow her on social media:

facebook.com/ShelleyKassianAuthor

twitter.com/@shelleykassian

instagram.com/shelleykassian

pinterest.com/shelleykassian

amazon.com/author/shelleykassian

goodreads.com/shelley_kassian

bookbub.com/authors/shelley-kassian

CPSIA information can be obtained
at www.ICGtesting.com
Printed in the USA
LVHW04s2308280518
578821LV00001B/34/P

9 780995 968059